Her mind had turned the thought over and over, trying to come up with a plausible explanation as to why her name would be on a hit list.

Nothing seemed reasonable. There was no explanation as to why anyone would want her dead.

Rachel kept an arm around her son, Aidan, as they drove farther and farther away from the world she was familiar with, traveling south on back roads she didn't recognize.

She turned to Jack. "Where are you taking us?"

His expression remained neutral. "Somewhere safe. We'll be going to the Iron, Inc. headquarters. It's not much farther away."

"Iron, Inc.?"

"We're an elite security firm. You'll be safe at our headquarters. No one gets in or out without our knowledge. The president could stay there and we wouldn't have to beef up security."

His words reminded her about the reality of the situation. "I can't even think straight."

"It's a lot to compr

"I'm...scared."

Jack gave her

Rachel closed
crumbled arou

Books by Christy Barritt

Love Inspired Suspense

Keeping Guard
The Last Target

CHRISTY BARRITT

loves stories and has been writing them for as long as she can remember. She gets her best ideas when she's supposed to be paying attention to something else—like in a workshop or while driving down the road.

The second book in her Squeaky Clean Mystery series, *Suspicious Minds,* won the inspiration category of the 2009 Daphne du Maurier Award for Excellence in Suspense and Mystery. She's also the co-author of *Changed: True Stories of Finding God in Christian Music.*

When she's not working on books, Christy writes articles for various publications. She's also a weekly feature writer for the *Virginian-Pilot* newspaper, the worship leader at her church and a frequent speaker at various writers groups, women's luncheons and church events.

She's married to Scott, a teacher and funny man extraordinaire. They have two sons, two dogs and a houseplant named Martha.

To learn more about her, visit her website at www.christybarritt.com.

THE
LAST
TARGET

Christy Barritt

Love Inspired

Recycling programs
for this product may
not exist in your area.

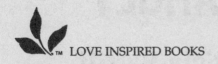

™ LOVE INSPIRED BOOKS

ISBN-13: 978-0-373-44458-8

THE LAST TARGET

Copyright © 2011 by Christy Barritt

www.LoveInspiredBooks.com

Printed in U.S.A.

My God is my rock, in whom I take refuge, my shield and the horn of my salvation. He is my stronghold, my refuge and my savior—from violent men you save me.
—*2 Samuel* 22:3

This book is dedicated to all the military who serve our country both abroad and here on our home turf. Thank you and your families for your dedication, sacrifices and courage.

ONE

Rachel Reynolds scanned the playground for any signs of trouble. Unsupervised children. Bullies. Swarming insects.

None. Just another day at the park for a dozen or so moms with their toddlers.

Her gaze shot back to her son, four-year-old Aidan, who was playing on the other side of the waist-high fence, not even ten feet away. He climbed up the plastic steps of the slide—the tallest one at the park—and stopped at the top.

"Look at me, Mommy!" His wide, brown eyes connected with hers and glowed with satisfaction.

Rachel waved and wiped at the perspiration on her forehead. Even under the shade of the pine tree, the summer heat still felt sweltering. "I'm watching, honey."

Just as he propelled himself down the slide, something hot whizzed past her arm. The smell of acid filled her nostrils. Pain sliced into her skin.

"Get down!" A man shoved her to the ground, his body shielding hers. He reached into his jacket and pulled out a gun. His mouth went to a wire at his wrist. "We've got shots fired. I repeat, shots have been fired."

Shots fired? Aidan. She had to get Aidan.

She raised her head up, gaze darting around the playground. Mobs of children and their mothers fled the park, screams filling the air. Where was Aidan?

Her gaze stopped at the slide. Aidan had climbed to the top again. She had to get him, to keep him safe.

"Aidan! Aidan!" She twisted her body, desperate to get away from the man who'd thrown her out of harm's way. Her fingers clawed at the grass. Her legs thrashed.

Her screams caught in her throat as a man approached the slide and grabbed Aidan. Her son's tear-filled gaze shot toward her, big eyes pleading for help. His arms reached for her just as the man who'd snatched him disappeared into the thick foliage of the woods.

A guttural cry rose from Rachel. "Aidan!" She pounded on the chest of the man shielding her as tears pushed their way out. The other man was getting away...with her son.

"That's one of my men who took your son. He'll keep him safe."

Her heart slowed a moment. "One of your men? Who are you?"

"I'll explain once you're safe."

Safe. She had felt safe only moments ago. That was pretty much all she wanted in life—to, as a single mom, provide a stable home for her son. In the blink of an eye, that life had been turned upside down.

What was going on? Why had someone opened fire at a playground? Were they crazy? She prayed no one was injured.

She needed to thank the men who'd saved her and Aidan and then retreat home. Lock her doors. Call the police. File a report.

"We need to lay low for a couple more minutes before I can get you out of here," the man said.

How had this man known there would be gunfire at the park today? Tension pinched her muscles. How had he gotten to her just in time? He'd known the shooting was going to happen, she realized. She felt the blood drain from her face.

What if he wasn't one of the good guys at all? She had to get away. Get Aidan.

The man's large frame easily overpowered her, though. What could she do? She ran through everything she'd learned in self-defense class. She had to use the weapons God had naturally given her.

Before she could reconsider, she pulled her elbow back and jabbed the man in the eye. "Get off me!"

As he blanched, she clawed the grass, pulling herself to safety.

Too late. The man grabbed her wrist and pulled her back. "Are you crazy?"

Eyes wide with terror, she shook her head. "No, you're crazy if you think I'm going anywhere with you. Get away from me!"

She tried to sock him in the jaw, but his strong grip clamped down on her wrist. "Listen to me a minute. Your uncle sent me."

She paused. "My uncle?"

"Vice Admiral Harris."

Her world began spinning.

"I'll explain everything. But right now, I've got to get you to safety." The man's iron-like hand gripped her arm. "Come on, we've got to get you out of here."

If Rachel wanted her safe life back, she had no choice but to trust this stranger. But the very thought caused fear to pulse through her.

Jack Sergeant scanned the park for the gunman. The shot had come from the woods behind him. That meant he'd have to get Rachel Reynolds to the waiting SUV with only his body as a shield. A few pines trees would offer measly protection against a bullet. At this point, they had little choice.

Rachel trembled in his grasp. Blood blurred across her

skin. Fear seemed to seize her breaths. If only he'd arrived at the park five minutes earlier; maybe they wouldn't be in this situation.

He'd think about that later. Now, he had to get the sweet-smelling woman out of here in one piece. He would have never guessed the gunman to be this aggressive or Rachel this stubborn.

"Rachel." He looked down at her wide, perfectly sculpted brown eyes. Finally, her gaze locked with his. "On the count of three, we're going to run toward the street. You'll be in front, I'll be behind you. Got it?"

She nodded, but apprehension showed in her shifting gaze. She was scared. She should be. This wasn't a game. Lives were in danger.

Another shot whizzed above them. They had to move and fast. He'd never forgive himself if something happened to her or her son.

"One." He shifted to the side, in position to lunge.

A small cry escaped from Rachel.

"Two." He tensed, ready to spring.

"Three!" He rushed to his feet, grabbed Rachel, pushed her in front of him and charged across the grass. A bullet splintered the tree beside them.

They sprinted toward the street at the park's entrance. Jack's body blocked Rachel. He was a good foot taller than her, and her strides couldn't meet his. He grabbed her elbow, propelling her onward.

Only a few more feet. He looked at the street, now cleared of cars. Where were his men?

In front of him, sweat glistened over Rachel's face. She pulled in ragged breaths. Her arms trembled beneath his grasp.

Another bullet panged into a brown metal sign. Rachel

gasped, froze for a moment. That had been close, mere feet away. Jack put his arm around her waist, urged her forward.

An SUV pulled to a screeching halt in front of them. The door opened and one of his men motioned to them. The air electrified as another shot rang out. Jack grabbed Rachel, swung her into his arms and slid her into the backseat. He shoved in after her and slammed the door.

Another bullet pierced the glass behind them as they squealed away. Jack could feel Rachel's heart hammering into his chest. As soon as she spotted her son on the floor, she reached for him. "Aidan!"

The car swerved again and sent all of them crashing into the door. The shooters were still on their trail. Jack and his men had to lose them, get Rachel and Aidan to safety.

"Hugs later." Jack reached over them. "Right now, seat belts on and heads down." He jerked the seat belts across them and clicked the buckles in place. Once they were secure and hunkered down, Jack grabbed his gun and looked out the back window. Two SUVs trailed them.

Another shot hit the back windshield, shattering it this time. Luke Black, the driver, swerved, and their SUV skittered close to the ditch beside them. The vehicle righted before zigzagging down the road in an attempt to avoid the gunfire behind them. Veins popped out on Luke's temple, and he had a white-knuckled grip on the steering wheel.

"We've got to lose them, Luke!"

"I'm trying." He took a quick left turn onto a busy Virginia Beach street. They charged through the yellow light at an intersection. The pursuing vehicles darted behind them. Two bystander cars skidded to a halt to avoid a crash.

Luke swerved again, this time onto a road that led away from the rush-hour congestion. The SUV nudged their bumper. Mark Denton, the other agent, stuck his gun out the window and fired, catching the front tire of one of the SUVs pursuing them. The vehicle jolted onto its side and rolled off the road. Rachel screamed and clung to her son.

Where did this road lead? Jack thought quickly until a plan settled in his mind. He glanced at his watch. "Go to the drawbridge!" It was scheduled to open on the hour. If they could get there and get across it before the SUV behind them, they might escape.

Rachel looked up with wide eyes. "The drawbridge? Are you crazy?"

Maybe. But it was their only chance. "You've got to trust me."

"I don't even know you!"

"I'm Jack Sergeant."

"FBI?"

The glass shattered on the window beside him. He threw himself over Rachel and Aidan, shielding them from flying glass and bullets.

"No, but I've been hired to protect you."

"Why in the world do I need protection?"

"Because your name was found on a hit list. Everyone else is—" He glanced at Aidan and then mouthed the word *dead*.

By the stark white appearance of Rachel's face, she got the message loud and clear. She ducked and placed herself over Aidan, kissing the top of his head.

The drawbridge waited ahead of them. Red stoplights flashed on either side of it, and a line of cars had already begun braking in front of them.

"The gates are going down!" Luke yelled.

"We can make it," Jack said, adrenaline charging through him. "Step on it!"

The SUV swerved into the opposite lane, charging forward toward the opening bridge.

"Hold on tight," he told Rachel. He pulled his own seat belt over him as they crashed through the gates. He prayed to God that they'd make it.

TWO

The bridge split open. The side closest to them rose like a ramp. The SUV accelerated.

Rachel closed her eyes and held her breath. *Lord, be with us.*

Rachel waited for the crash. The impact of water. An explosion. Pain.

The SUV flew up the bridge arm. At the end, it caught air. They hung suspended a moment. Finally, their tires hit the metal grates on the other side. The vehicle bounced against the bridge before squealing down the road.

Rachel sucked in a deep breath, her hands trembling. They'd survived. Barely.

She hugged her son. "Are you okay, honey?"

Aidan looked up, his big brown eyes filled with emotion. "That was cool! Can we do it again sometime?"

Rachel sighed and felt some tension drain from her. "Absolutely not." She ruffled his hair and closed her eyes only a moment before glancing at Jack. "Did we lose them?" *And exactly who is "them"?*

Jack glanced behind them. "For now. But we're not out of danger yet."

Rachel squeezed Aidan and sunk down in the leather seat. Whoever this Jack guy was, he'd just saved her life and the life of her son. She kissed the top of Aidan's head again and held him against her chest.

She glanced over at Jack, taking her first good look at him. The man was dark-haired and broad-shouldered with a finely chiseled, square face. He wore a white button-up shirt with the sleeves rolled to his elbows. Striking blue eyes softened his otherwise macho features. Those very eyes seemed to be assessing her as they cruised down the wooded road through the swampland of Virginia Beach.

Sucking in a breath, she looked out the front window. Ominous clouds hovered in the distance as if even nature knew about the danger they were in. She felt like she'd been pulled into a different world, like Alice going down the rabbit hole.

Jack touched her arm where the bullet had grazed her. "You'll need to have that looked at."

Now that he mentioned it, her arm was throbbing. The bullet had barely grazed her, but her sleeve was soaked with blood. The sight made her feel woozy, so she looked away. "I'll be fine."

Aidan turned his big brown eyes up to her again. "What happened, Mommy?"

She patted his back. "Just a little boo-boo."

Jack reached into the back of the SUV and grabbed a first aid kit. He searched through it before pulling out some gauze and bandages. She flinched at the feeling of his fingers—although surprisingly gentle—on her skin. She didn't know if her reaction was from the pain or from the electricity that zipped through her. She was comfortable with neither.

As Jack wrapped her arm, Rachel tried to keep her expression neutral, to hide her pain. But the wound burned and her arm ached. Things could have turned out much worst, she reminded herself. She could be dead.

Her mind had turned the thought over and over, trying to come up with a plausible explanation as to why her name would be on a hit list. Nothing seemed reasonable. There was no explanation as to why anyone would want her dead. She was a widow whose husband had died in the Middle East while serving in the military, and an only child whose parents had been killed in an auto accident. She lived a mostly private life and stayed out of other people's business.

Questions bounced through her mind. There'd be time to demand answers soon, but not now when Aidan was so alert and perceptive. Right now, she had to concentrate on survival.

Rachel kept an arm around Aidan as they drove farther and farther away from the world she was familiar with, traveling south on back roads she didn't recognize. Aidan looked out the window and sang to himself. Kids were so resilient, much more than they got credit for, she mused. His naivety was a blessing, especially at this very moment.

When she was sure Aidan wasn't listening, she turned to Jack. "Where are you taking us?"

His expression remained neutral. "Somewhere safe."

"That's kind of vague."

Some intensity left Jack's eyes and was replaced with… compassion, perhaps? "We'll be going to the Iron, Inc., headquarters. It's not much farther away."

"Iron, Inc.?"

"We're an elite security firm. We get contracts from the military and law-enforcement organizations. Most people who work with us just call us Eyes."

"Exactly what kind of contracts do you get?"

"Guarding ambassadors, training security teams, executing top-secret missions."

"You do all of those things, and you've been hired to protect me?" The truth tried to settle on her, but reality seemed too much like fiction right now. This couldn't be happening.

He offered a clipped nod. "We have."

"And what exactly do you do for Eyes?"

"I am Eyes. I started the organization four years ago. You'll be safe at our headquarters. No one gets in or out without our knowledge. The whole place is protected with a twelve-foot fence and armed guards. The president of the United States could stay there and we wouldn't have to beef up security."

His words reminded her about the reality of the situation. She pinched the bridge of her nose. "I can't even think straight."

"It's a lot to comprehend."

"I'm…scared."

Jack gave her a terse nod. "You should be."

Rachel closed her eyes as life as she knew it crumbled around her.

Hope for the best; prepare for the worst.

Jack silently repeated his mantra as they pulled through the gates into the Eyes headquarters. Only, as he liked to say it, *Pray* for the best; prepare for the worst.

The best would be that the terrorists wouldn't guess that his team had taken Rachel to Eyes; that the terrorist group Apaka would be thrown off Rachel's trail and evidence from the park would lead to the group's capture. The worst would be that Apaka knew where they'd gone, and the terrorists were on their way here to try and finish what they'd started.

Apaka was ruthless. They were based primarily out of the former Soviet state of Uzbekistan, but they'd grown to infiltrate much of the Middle East and even had some cells in the United States. Their goal was destroy life in the United States as its citizens knew it, using whatever means possible. Even more, they were fear-mongers. Whatever they could do to spread anxiety throughout the country—the world, for that matter—they would do.

As the vehicle pulled to a stop, Jack opened the bullet-pierced door and extended a hand to Rachel. The woman's pale skin and dull eyes made her look dazed, frightened. His heart squeezed at the sight. To be ripped from a comfortable life and thrown into this situation would overwhelm anyone.

He squeezed her uninjured arm as she slipped out. "You'll be safe here. I promise."

He'd only broken one promise in his life, and he'd vowed to never do that again. He'd broken his promise to love his wife the way she deserved. He had to live every day with the fact that she'd gone running to another man's arms as a result. An image of Jennifer flashed in his mind and his heart panged with sadness at his past mistakes.

Fat raindrops splashed from the sky as he walked with Rachel to the other side of the car and opened the door for her. Rachel reached for her sleeping son but winced in pain as she tried to lift him.

Jack stepped forward. "Let me."

She hesitated and then stepped back, as if realizing she had no choice. Carefully, Jack took the sleeping preschooler from the vehicle and laid him against his shoulder. He felt Rachel watching his every move, as if she didn't trust him. She had no reason to trust him yet. He was a stranger to her, though Jack knew her long before today.

Once Aidan rested snugly on his shoulder, Jack nodded for Rachel to follow as they raced through the rain and entered the main lodge. Inside awaited a huge lobby donned with two fireplaces and multiple couches and tables. They veered off down a hallway with plain white walls and simple, nondescript doors. One turn later they reached the sleeping quarters.

"This is where you'll stay," he told her.

The suite boasted a tiny living area with an industrial-looking couch, table and two chairs. Beyond that was a bedroom with two twin beds made up with plain navy-blue coverlets on each side and a tiny bathroom in the middle.

Rachel nodded, her face void of an opinion. "Why don't you just put Aidan on the bed so he can finish his nap?"

Slowly, he laid the boy on a twin bed, listening for the easy breathing that ensured he still slept. When he was sure he hadn't woken the boy, he stepped back, his heart lurching for some unknown reason at the sight of the child. Jack didn't want the kid's innocence to be ripped from him, but he was afraid that was just what would happen. The boy had already been through so much, losing his father and grandparents before he was even born. Jack would see to it that he didn't lose his mother also.

"You're pretty good at that. You must have lots of experience."

Rachel's voice jolted him. He glanced over and saw her examining him, an arm crossed over her chest. "Just a couple of nieces and nephews." Who he rarely got to see because of how far away they lived. Still, he loved being with them whenever possible.

"I want to talk to my uncle."

"He's out of the country right now, but he's going to call you tomorrow. He's in the middle of a project right now and can't get away."

"I see."

He stared at her another minute, trying to read her expression. Reading women never was his strength. Thankfully, the medic on duty came down the hall at that moment. Though Jack had bandaged her arm in the SUV, it had only been a temporary fix. Rachel needed some butterfly bandages to hold the wound together.

Jack watched as the medic bandaged Rachel's arm. Until today he'd only seen Rachel from a distance. She looked even more beautiful up close. Thick, dark, glossy hair fell in waves around her face. Her dark, big eyes spoke volumes about her thoughts and intelligence. And the woman was definitely intelligent. She was the founder and director of the nonprofit Operation 26 Letters.

Through her organization, Rachel brought comfort to so many members of the military by simply encouraging people to write letters to them. Operation 26 Letters had even been profiled on a national news program once. What had started as a simple operation with a handful of volunteers had turned into a huge undertaking that reached thousands.

Rachel worked with volunteers from across the country, not only recruiting them to write letters to military personnel overseas, but they'd also grown to put together care packages to send to the troops and to provide Thanksgiving and Christmas baskets for spouses and families at home. She'd turned her grief over losing her husband into a true ministry by letting those who served their country know that they truly weren't ever forgotten, and Jack had always admired her for that.

Yes, Jack had known a lot more about Rachel even before today. He'd heard about her firsthand from the first person she'd ever written letters to, before Operation 26 Letters was even a dream.

There were things that Jack could never tell her about his past, about her past, about how they were connected. Or could he? Would Rachel understand if she knew he'd read the personal letters she used to write to her husband? Or would she despise him if she knew?

Jack put those thoughts aside as the medic finished bandaging her up and left. He drew in a deep breath. He dreaded this conversation, knowing it would rock her world. "We need to talk."

Rachel glanced at Aidan's sleeping figure and nodded

toward the front room. "Let's go in there so we don't wake him up."

She settled on the couch and Jack perched on a chair across from her. He locked his gaze on hers. "I'm sure you have lots of questions."

"I hardly know what to ask."

"Let me try to explain." He glanced at his hands before locking in his gaze with hers again. "Recently, a Navy SEAL team captured a terrorist by the name of Abram Titov. He's a part of the terrorist group Apaka. If you watch the news, you've heard of them. They're not the largest or most powerful terrorist group, but they're nothing to blink an eye at either. In Titov's pocket, we found a list of names and addresses. We began investigating the people on the list, trying to figure out what their connection was with each other and with Titov."

Rachel nodded. "Okay."

"The links didn't appear easily. In fact, they hardly appeared at all." Jack shifted in his chair. "We did find one thing, though."

Rachel's face still looked painfully white. "Go on."

"Rachel, everyone on the list is now dead. Murdered." The lines around his eyes tightened. "Everyone except one person."

Her eyes widened. "Me." The word was so soft it was barely audible.

Jack nodded. "You. We've got to figure out why they're trying to kill you before—"

"Before they succeed," she finished.

Jack nodded and watched as Rachel's face went into her hands. He knew the past three hours had rocked her world. He prayed he could ease her fears. But more than that, he prayed that he could keep her alive.

Apaka's reach was deep, like an inky darkness that spread

wherever it pleased, infiltrating the toughest forts through the smallest cracks. How long could he hold off the darkness before it slithered here to find her?

He prayed that the answer was "forever."

THREE

This had to be a dream, a nightmare. Why would a terrorist be carrying around her name?

Somehow, Jack appeared on the couch beside her. His heavy, strong hand rested on her shoulder. "I know this is a lot to take in. Are you okay?"

Rachel tried to nod, but couldn't. Everyone on the list was dead but her? That's what she'd thought Jack had said in the car, but she'd hoped she'd misunderstood. She'd convinced herself that's what had happened.

Dead.

The word seemed to echo in her mind, its reverberations causing her trembles to intensify. Where did she start with the questions? "Dead...how?"

"Different means, none that would obviously connect the crimes. One in a carjacking. Another in a home invasion. One person was in a car accident—the brake lines were cut. Another was robbed and shot while in a gas station."

"How many? How many were on the list?"

"Six, including you."

"Tell me about them, the people on the list." She needed more information so she could try to make sense of the news. Facts were the only comfort she had at the moment, her only hope of feeling somewhat grounded.

Jack's hand slipped from her shoulder. "One was an

entomologist in Montana. Another was a political science professor in Iowa. There was an industrial scientist in Texas, a Kansas wheat farmer and a molecular engineer in New Jersey."

"And me." She blinked rapidly. "Why would I be on that list? It just doesn't make sense. Why would a terrorist target me? Why would they target any of those people?"

"That's what we're trying to figure out. We're dedicated to keeping you safe until we have the answers we need."

She looked around the room, at this new place, so foreign to her and Aidan. "Why here? Why you?"

"Your uncle charged me to personally keep guard over you."

"No offense, but you're not military or FBI or CIA. I've never even heard of you or this organization."

"I've got a good track record for keeping people safe."

Her son's face flashed in her mind. She glanced into the next room at his sweet figure, so angelic as he slumbered. She'd do whatever it took to make sure he was safe. She turned back to Jack and studied his chiseled face, his stony expression offset by those blue eyes. Now that she got a better look at the man, she thought he might be slightly familiar. Where would she have met Jack Sergeant before, though?

"We'd like to go over some questions with you. Also, I'll need your cell phone."

She reached for her purse, that she still had only because it was in a messenger bag that had been slung over her chest. "Can't I just turn it off?"

Jack shook his head. "We're dealing with some sophisticated terrorists. These aren't men in caves who are cut off from the world. These are men who've got an endless supply of money, resources and connections."

She handed the phone to him. Aidan would miss it more than she would. He'd taken to playing the various games she had on the phone whenever he needed something to occupy himself.

"We'll get you a new cell phone so you can have it on hand at all times, in case you need it. I'd advise against calling anyone you know, though. Your friends' lines could be monitored as well."

Other than her Uncle Arnold, who would she call? Her best friend, Kelly, who was also the assistant director of Operation 26 Letters, was out of the country on a month-long mission in Mexico. She supposed she should call the president of the Board of Directors for her nonprofit. Someone would need to take over operations there for a few days until this mess was taken care of. And she'd need to call Aidan's preschool.

She had no family left to call. She was an only child and her parents were dead. Her husband's, Andrew's, family had never really been interested in either their son or grandson, for that matter. She wished she did have family to call. She wished her husband was still alive to take care of her and Aidan, to protect them. Life hadn't worked out the way she'd planned or hoped. She hadn't gotten her happily-ever-after. She'd accepted that. But now this curveball happened.

Jack motioned to a guard outside the door and instructed him to bring him a few items from his office. Rachel leaned back against the couch and studied Jack as the guard retreated. He seemed the perfect mix of soldier and CEO, with his muscular, strapping build and his upright, serious demeanor.

"You really are the big man around here, aren't you?"

He raised an eyebrow. "If we succeed or we fail, it falls on my shoulders. As the old saying goes, the buck stops here."

"I usually prefer to think that if I succeed or fail, it's all a part of God's plan. I do my best and I let Him do the rest. Helps me to sleep better at night."

"I can't argue with that. Trusting God gets me through my days."

Rachel nodded. Knowing that the man who was charged with guarding her life and the life of her son trusted in God comforted her and made her feel a sense of confidence in him.

Jack leaned toward her, his elbows propped on his knees. "Rachel, I'm going to have to ask you some hard questions."

"I understand. I have nothing to hide. I just want this to be over with."

He nodded. "Good. Let me start with this. Do you have any idea why someone would want you dead?"

She'd been asking herself the same question for the past three hours. The only possible connection she could establish was her husband. He'd been a Navy SEAL. They were known for doing some top-secret operations, operations that sometimes had worldwide effects, operations where they were faceless, where they never got the credit. But they'd been the ones on the frontlines, the ones changing history.

But her husband had been dead for four years and she knew relatively nothing of his work. And if her husband's work was the connection, what about the other names on the list? Did everyone have some connection with the SEALs? Certainly Jack and his men would have put that together by now if it were there.

"My husband's career perhaps?"

"Your husband was our first thought also. The problem is that none of the other people had any connection with the Navy SEALs."

The guard came back into the room at that moment and handed Jack a briefcase. Jack reached into it and pulled out a folder. "I'm going to show you a copy of the list and see if any of the names are familiar to you."

He placed in front of her a copy of a stained paper with

hastily written names scribbled across it. Just seeing her name jotted there made her heart pulse erratically. The realism of the situation hit her even harder, feeling like a punch in the gut.

She looked the names over, searching her brain for something—anything—that would trigger a connection. "No, none of the names are familiar. Can you tell me about them? Who are these people? Maybe that will spark something."

He reviewed the names, but it was just like he had told her earlier. They were all from different parts of the United States with different ages, different incomes and different careers. The names appeared to be random, but Rachel knew there had to be some connection.

Jack leaned toward her, his eyes serious and dazzling blue. Every time she looked at them, she seemed to get drawn in. She looked away, concentrated on his mouth instead.

"I'm sorry, Jack. I wish I could help…"

He leaned back in his seat, and Rachel could tell he was disappointed. So was she. She wished more than anything that she did have some answers, that just seeing the list had made a light bulb turn on and given them a solution that would end this nightmare.

For the next hour they reviewed where she'd been raised, her family, her education, seemingly mundane details of her life. When they finished, she let her head fall back against the couch. She just needed something to make sense. Maybe then she'd have some hope for a happy ending.

"I can tell you're exhausted, Rachel. We can finish this in the morning." The soft, compassionate look had returned to Jack's eyes.

She appreciated his courtesy, but now wasn't the time. She didn't move. Sure, she was tired and she'd love nothing more than to get some rest—in her own bed, in her own home. But there wouldn't be such thing as true "rest" until she felt safe again. They had to keep going.

Rachel pinched the skin between her eyes. She had to stay calm, to ward away the anxiety that tried desperately to grip her. Finally, she dropped her hand and opened her eyes with what she hoped conveyed renewed energy. "Let's keep going."

Jack laced his fingers in front of him as if trying to look casual. It didn't work. "Tell me about your nonprofit, Rachel."

"My nonprofit?" What could it have to do with any of this? "I just encourage people to write letters to the military stationed overseas. It's hardly anything controversial."

"Have you had any problems with it? Any volunteers who've been acting strangely? Any members of the military who became obsessed with the person who was writing them? Any suspicious letters that came across your desk maybe?"

"There are people who hate the military so therefore they hate us, too. They've sent some nasty letters and emails. Once we even had people picketing outside our office in Virginia Beach."

"Did you save any of that correspondence?"

"All of it."

"I'll need to see it."

"No problem."

"Anything else? Any other people who have acted suspiciously? Even something that might not seem important could be."

She searched her brain for something that should set off an alarm. Nothing emerged. Sure, she'd had volunteers who'd dropped the ball and hadn't followed through with their commitment. Sure, there had even been a couple of romances develop after volunteers became pen pals with their assignments. But no one in particular stood out as suspicious.

She sat up straight. No one in particular except...

Jack leaned toward her. "What is it?"

"I'm sure it's nothing." She leaned back into the couch and waved away the thought.

"Why don't you let me decide that."

She licked her lips, unsure of the wisdom in even mentioning her thought. Then she thought of Aidan. She had to keep him safe, and to do that Jack and his men needed to explore every possibility. "There is one man who's on the board for the organization. He has a bit of an edge to him. But—"

"What's his name?"

Her face flushed. "George Anderson."

Jack's stony expression seemed to shift for a moment. As quickly as whatever emotion it was passed through his gaze, his intense look returned. "We'll look into him, just to be safe."

Her world felt like it was spinning. Could George be behind these attacks? It didn't seem possible. "He served with my husband as a Navy SEAL. After Andrew died, George made an effort to help me out around the house some—trimming trees, cleaning gutters, things like that. But what possible connection could he have with this list?"

"Rachel…"

The way Jack said her name made her realize that he was holding something back, trying to protect her. It was too late to feel safe now. "Just tell me, Jack. You don't have to beat around the bush. I can handle it."

"Rachel, there's a good chance that whoever shot you at the park today missed on purpose."

Her heart seemed to skip a beat. "Why would they do that?"

"Maybe because they know you. Maybe because they couldn't bring themselves to hurt you."

She shook her head. "That still doesn't make any sense. I'm not following you…"

"Nobody else survived an attempt on their life. Only you. There's got to be a reason for that."

"Nobody I know would be affiliated with Apaka."

"Are you sure?"

"I'm sure." She sounded more confident than she felt.

Jack sighed and leaned back in his chair. "Then maybe you know something. Maybe they want to keep you alive to get information that only you have."

"What information would I have? Information on how to write compelling letters to military personnel stationed overseas? How to potty-train a child? There's nothing I know that they could possibly want."

Jack seemed to sense her rising anxiety. He placed his hand on her knee and waited until she made eye contact to speak. "I understand this is a lot to process, Rachel."

Rachel's throat went dry and she stood. She only wanted to hug Aidan, to lock the door to their room and throw away the key. It seemed the only semblance of safety she could think of at the moment.

But was it the situation that had her feeling flustered, or was it the jolt of electricity that coursed through her at Jack's touch?

It didn't matter. Both were dangerous. She had to hold on to whatever security she had at the moment. She had no control of the terrorists. But she could get away from Jack Sergeant before she lost control of her fluttering heart.

FOUR

Aidan called out for his mother from the next room. Jack watched as Rachel's face seemed to flush with relief. Maybe this had been too much for her. Maybe he should have waited until she rested some before asking the questions.

Still, Rachel had a trouper's attitude. She'd held up amazingly well considering the circumstances. Even the toughest person would crumble under the weight of what she'd just learned.

"Let me get Aidan." Rachel rose. "He may be scared not knowing where he is."

Jack wasn't going to leave Rachel alone. Not right now. He planned on staying by her side as much as possible until the people behind the threat on her life were either dead or behind bars.

Instead, Jack stared at the mess of notes in front of him. A mess of notes, but no answers. Just more ideas. Ideas didn't seem good enough at the moment. Right now, he wanted answers. And he wanted to keep his promises, including one he'd made four years ago.

He never thought this day would come, the day that he and Rachel would both become characters on the same stage. But here they were, thrown together in the most harrowing of circumstances. Not only had he been hired to protect her—a task he'd see to personally—but he was also fulfilling a promise he'd whispered to a man on his deathbed.

That was all Andrew had asked of Jack before life had faded from him. Make sure his wife and baby were okay. He probably would have asked that of any of his comrades who had been there with him on his deathbed. Although Jack and Andrew had been friends, they hadn't been that kind of friends. But Jack had been the one who was there to hear Andrew's last desperate plea for his family. It was a shame that Andrew had asked the one person who was never supposed to have known him, though. Jack had been undercover, even used an alias while on assignment. Even worse, Andrew had been the main crux of his mission. The government had feared he'd been selling secrets to the enemy. Andrew had been cleared of those suspicions, but still, an invisible weight pressed on Jack's shoulders at the thought.

Jack heard Rachel talking in soothing tones to Aidan in the next room. He knew even before today that Rachel was a good mother. He knew she was patient and loving, yet disciplined and firm. Jack had seen her from his place in the background. Not very often. He hadn't wanted to scare her by being a shadow in her life. But he kept tabs on her, made sure she was okay. He'd made sure to donate to Rachel's nonprofit. He'd made sure she had no unmet needs. Everything had been going well, so smoothly...until today.

He looked at his notes again. George Anderson.

He remembered George from his time working alongside the SEALs team in Afghanistan. Had George and Rachel ever dated? Why did the thought of it make Jack tense?

He knew—it was because George was a hothead and a hotshot. He wanted to do things that put the whole SEALs team and everyone else around them in danger.

But was he a killer? Could he secretly be working for Apaka?

Jack knew the reasons why someone would be lured into working for a terrorist organization. They would probably pay a hefty dollar for the right information about where the U.S. troops were headed next for battle. The traitor could have provided that information, taken a large sum of money and then gotten out of the military.

Apaka looked just like anyone else. That's what made them dangerous. They blended in. Many were homegrown. Their agents could be anyone.

He glanced toward the other room and saw that Rachel was still occupied with Aidan. He picked up his phone and made a call to Luke.

"Luke, I need you to look into someone named George Anderson. Find out where he's been for the past six months, if he's traveled anywhere. Look into his checking account. I need to find out if he's our man."

"Yes, sir."

He glanced back again and saw Rachel stroking her son's hair, a gentle smile on her face. For some reason, the image made his heart lurch. He looked away, staring at his notes again and remembering the conversation at hand. "How about the park? Did you find any evidence there? Any clues as to who the shooter was?"

"I'm talking to the local police right now. Thanks to a call from the Department of Defense we've got their full cooperation. No one at the park seems to have seen anything, however, except a mass of people scattering for cover."

Jack replayed the incident again. Why hadn't the shooter gotten Rachel? Why had he spared her after killing everyone else on the list? He was sure of one thing—it wasn't an accident she was still alive. But he was also sure they weren't finished with her yet. Now he just had to figure out why. In figuring that out, he may also figure out who was behind these attacks.

His men had been working nonstop on this case since Jack had gotten the phone call yesterday from Vice Admiral Harris, his contact at the U.S. Department of Defense and Rachel's uncle. He had analysts looking over the list, searching phone records, examining backgrounds. He had strategists plotting various ways to catch the men behind the attacks. He had security specialists figuring out ways to up safety measures here at Eyes.

Yes, their headquarters were more closely guarded than the White House, as he liked to say. He hadn't lied about that. But still, to not make mistakes, they needed to reevaluate, find any areas of weakness.

Some of the best men at the Department of Defense and CIA examined that list after it had been discovered two days ago, and all had been unable to determine the links between the names. They could only hope that Rachel could provide some information that would give them a lead. Without any insight from Rachel, they might not ever figure out the reasons behind these murders. She was their source for answers…but Jack's main concern was keeping her and Aidan safe.

His thoughts went back to his final night in Afghanistan. He pictured the explosion that had rocked his world. He could see Andrew's lifeless body. He'd pulled him from the Hummer and tried to revive him. It was too late. He was never supposed to have hit that improvised explosive device.

Jack had been the one who'd told Andrew to go to Kabul. Jack had wanted to trail him, to see who he was meeting. He'd wanted to catch Andrew in the act of being a traitor. Instead, Jack had led him straight to his death.

If Rachel learned the truth about what happened that night, how would she feel about Jack? She would never trust him. After all, how could she forgive him for the death of her husband and her son's father?

The thought pressed on him as he looked once more at the list.

* * *

"Where are we, Mommy?"

Rachel pulled Aidan into her arms. "This is where we're going to be staying for a few days. It's kind of like a hotel." She couldn't let anything happen to her son. She'd protect him, even if it meant staying here at the Eyes headquarters and abandoning her life.

"Like the time we stayed at the beach and ate pizza and played in the waves?"

Rachel smiled. "Yes, kind of like that." Rachel wished she had a sweater to pull over her arms. She told herself it was the AC that had her quivering, but she knew the truth. Fear had invaded her and shaken her to the core. This all seemed like a nightmare that she needed to wake up from. The bandage across her arm proved that this situation was all too real, though.

Aidan's chin trembled. "Why did that man grab me from the slide?"

Rachel's heart panged, remembering her son's expression during the ordeal, remembering how helpless she felt. "I know that was scary. He was trying to help, though. There was a bad man in the park, and the good guy was trying to keep you away from him."

"A bad man?"

Rachel nodded.

"I thought you said monsters weren't real."

Her heart panged again. She didn't know what to say. Instead, she pulled her son into her arms again and rocked him back and forth. *Lord, I don't have the answers...help me.*

She opened her mouth, hoping the right words would pop out, when Aidan sighed and proclaimed, "I'm hungry."

Hungry. Jack had mentioned something about food. Maybe a good meal would be a perfect distraction for both herself and Aidan. She rose and reached for his hand. "Let's go get something to eat then."

Just seeing Jack on the phone in the next room caused the revelation about the list and the threat on her life to slam back into her mind. She studied him another minute, wondering again why he seemed familiar. Did Jack know Andrew? She felt confident there was something Jack wasn't telling her. His eyes had taken on a haunted look when Andrew's name had been mentioned.

Perhaps Jack had been a former SEAL. Maybe it didn't matter if Jack knew Andrew personally. SEALs—whether they knew each other or not—seemed to form an impenetrable camaraderie. They were closer than brothers. When one SEAL was lost, the whole community of special ops mourned for them. That had been evident at Andrew's funeral.

The day flashed into her mind and she squeezed her eyes shut, pushing the memories away. She didn't want to go there. Not now. She didn't want to think about Andrew and the questions she had about a few mysterious aspects of his life. She'd chosen to simply believe the best and put aside her questions.

Jack looked up at that moment and smiled at Aidan. "How's it going, buddy? Did you have a nice nap?"

Aidan nodded and rubbed his eyes. "I'm hungry."

"It just so happens that I have some macaroni and cheese coming up for you right now. Do you like mac and cheese?"

Aidan's eyes lit up. "It's my favorite."

At that moment, the guard knocked at the door and brought in several bags of food. He placed them on the coffee table that lay between them. Rachel helped Jack pull the food out and placed it before them. He'd ordered a variety, obviously not knowing what they liked. Rachel chose a ham-and-cheese sandwich for herself. She pulled the lid off of Aidan's food and set it before him. He quickly dug in.

"Does mac and cheese help you grow?" Aidan asked, looking at Jack. He already had orange, gooey cheese all over his lips and chin. "I want to be big and tall one day, just like you. Like a superhero."

Jack grinned. "Mac and cheese…the dinner of champions. That's what I like to say."

Rachel raised an eyebrow. Today of all days she wasn't going to argue about what her son ate. There were other issues to worry about. She took another bite of her sandwich, though she had to admit that nothing tasted good right now. She was just going through the motions, eating because she knew she had to in order to keep her energy.

Jack turned his gaze back to Rachel, his eyes serious again. "As soon as you're both finished, I'd like to show you around the headquarters. I hope you'll be comfortable here. Just not too comfortable."

Rachel knew what he was getting at. She had to remain on guard at all times, even within the security of the headquarters here. They were dealing with terrorists. Jack didn't need to spell it out for Rachel to realize the resources Apaka had. They'd do anything to finish what they started.

Rachel shivered.

Keep things normal, she reminded herself. She had to keep a cool head for Aidan's sake. She cleared her throat. "From what I've seen so far, it seems like quite the setup you have here."

Jack's gaze remained on her a moment too long. She almost felt like Jack could see right through the surface and knew her thoughts, her fears, her forced façade in front of her son. "I try to make it as much like home as possible," Jack finally said. "For many of the men here, this is like a second home. It's my only home, for that matter."

"Your family lives here then?" She was just asking to make conversation, she told herself. It was only fair that if she had to expose her entire life to this stranger then she should know something about him.

His eyes seemed to cloud at the question. "No family. It's easier that way."

Rachel nodded. "I'm sure." She wasn't sure how to take his statement. Was it easier this way because he didn't like to be tied down, or easier this way because there was less pressure to divide his time? Maybe both? It didn't matter. It wasn't her place to convince him otherwise. And, in some ways, maybe it was easier for people in the military to be single. At least, that's what she thought on her cynical days.

Jack's phone rang again. He looked at the screen before plucking it from his belt and putting it to his ear. His posture immediately went stiff. "Vice Admiral Harris. I understand. Yes, I will pass that on. Okay. Thanks."

Rachel tensed. What was the phone call about? Had they captured the person behind the shooting? Had someone else been hurt?

Jack turned to her with serious eyes. "That was your uncle. He's coming down to talk to you tomorrow."

"I thought he was out of the country."

"He was. He's back now. He cut his trip short."

"What's going on?"

"The Department of Defense just received a letter for you. When they opened it, they noticed a powdery substance inside. After the powder was cleared of being toxic, they read the letter."

"And?"

"It was a note to you from Apaka."

The blood drained from her face. "To me? With my name on it? What did it say?"

"It said 'We're not done yet.'"

FIVE

Rachel shoved her sandwich aside and leaned back against the couch. Nausea roiled in her gut. Why did it feel like just when things couldn't get worst, they did?

"It's our belief that Apaka doesn't know you're here," Jack said in an obvious attempt to comfort her.

"But they will, won't they? Eventually. They don't seem like the type to give up easily."

Jack's silence spoke volumes.

Rachel wiped the corners of her mouth, again trying to round up her thoughts. She glanced at Aidan and saw that he was preoccupied with a coloring page that had been placed in the bag with his food. "So, when did the first...the first... incident from the list...occur?"

"The list? Mommy, you like lists." Aidan popped his head up. So, he had been listening. She should have known better. Aidan's perceptiveness never ceased to amaze her.

She patted his hand. "You're right, honey. I do like lists. Grocery lists. To-do lists. Birthday lists." She and Jack exchanged a glance. *Not hit lists.*

When Aidan went back to coloring, Jack spoke. "Three months ago."

Rachel's skin went cold. Whoever was behind the attacks was acting swiftly. They'd eluded law enforcement by revealing no modus operandi. And if that terrorist hadn't been captured, her life would have ended also with no one thinking anything strange about it.

The other deaths had seemed random. Why had Apaka planned her ending by shooting her in a park? With the other deaths, it could seem like a robbery gone bad or like an accident even. The incident in the park today was nothing but malicious. There was no covering that up.

She shook her head, not able to think about it.

"Excuse me, Mister...Mister..."

"Jack. You can call me Jack."

"Excuse me, Mr. Jack. What's your superpower?" Aidan stared at Jack with large, curious eyes.

Jack raised a brow. "Superpower?"

Rachel licked her lips, so used to her son's superhero banter that she didn't realize how strange it may sound to others. "He thinks you're a superhero, and every superhero has a superpower."

"Can you leap tall buildings?"

Jack shook his head.

"Fly?"

"Only in a plane."

"Shoot webs from your hands?"

Jack leaned closer, a grin on his face. His demeanor had changed from all professional to warm in an instant. "You know, I actually can't tell you what my superpower is. It's a secret."

Aidan took the bait and grinned. "I bet you can become invisible."

Jack nudged the boy's chin affectionately. "I like your persistence."

Now that Aidan mentioned it, there was something about Jack Sergeant that reminded Rachel, a bit, of a superhero. He seemed strong, powerful and like he had a good heart, one that was bent on protecting the innocent.

The problem was that this wasn't a comic book or a movie. In real life, the superhero didn't always win.

Her heart twisted at the thought.

"How about we go and get some fresh air?" Jack suggested.

Fresh air sounded nice. Rachel nodded and rose. She took Aidan's hand and followed Jack out of the room and through the building. They stepped outside into the early evening sun, that still felt sweltering despite the earlier shower. A light breeze helped cool the air slightly.

They stepped off of the wooden porch and onto the grounds, which, other than being a paramilitary complex, were nice with plentiful grass, woods at the perimeter and water in the distance. If it weren't for the men running around in uniform, one might think the place was a vacation spot. Rachel already had thoughts of sitting on the porch to watch the sunset.

Too bad she knew better. Aidan didn't have to, though.

They stopped at a man-made lake and Aidan began throwing rocks in the water. While he was distracted, Rachel turned to Jack. "So, what's next? Do I just stay here until every member of Apaka is captured and behind bars? Because that feels a bit like a prison sentence. No offense. It's just that they might as well kill me if I'm going to spend the rest of my life without any freedom."

Jack glanced at Aidan, as if double-checking that he wasn't listening. "It won't be forever. But we will need your patience. Your safety is our first priority."

She kicked at a rock. "I appreciate that." She looked around at the campus of Eyes. "So you started this place? Why?"

"I saw ways of doing things more efficiently. I saw needs that weren't being met, gaps that needed to be filled, so I started dreaming. I like doing things my way."

"You sound like me."

They shared a smile.

"I'm proud of all of the men and women who work here. Our goal is simply to protect our country."

If they could protect an entire country, certainly they could protect her. Right? The tension didn't leave her, though. She didn't know if it would until Apaka was stopped.

She glanced at Aidan, throwing stones with all of his might. "So, who do you employ here? Ex-military?"

"Mostly ex-military. Some former law enforcement, CIA, FBI. Only the best. We do highly classified missions and act as government contractors. My men put their lives at risk. They don't get fancy funerals or big awards from the Pentagon. But what they do is valuable. I want to treat them accordingly. I pay what they deserve, but, as a result, I'm very selective about who I bring on."

Rachel's gaze scanned her surroundings, impeccably kept and deceitfully peaceful. She still half expected a bullet to come flying through the air at any moment. "This is where they do all their training?"

Jack nodded. "Pretty much. They stay in shape and train, learning new techniques and basically preparing for battle or whatever situation we're called into."

Rachel absorbed all of the new information. As the facts settled in her mind, she leaned down to grab a rock and attempted to skim it across the water.

"You're former military?"

He nodded.

"How'd you get into this line of work, Jack?"

"I wish I had a really admirable back story, but the truth is that I didn't know what I wanted to do after high school so I joined the military. Once I got in, I loved everything about it."

"So much so that you became a SEAL?"

"I was a SEAL."

"But you weren't on my husband's team?"

"No, I wasn't."

She narrowed her eyes. "What aren't you telling me?"

"I did work with your husband once, Rachel. But I wasn't on his SEAL team."

Her face looked still, uneasily calm. "You worked with Andrew?"

"We met a couple of times when I was stationed over in the Middle East." He glanced at her as if trying to read her expression. "He was a good man."

"Thank you." She threw another rock into the water. "Aidan has a lot of his father in him."

"I can see the resemblance."

Just over the lake, the sun was beginning to sink into the horizon. Now that she thought about it, she was exhausted. She needed some time alone to process everything that had happened today.

"You ready to go back inside?"

She nodded, and Jack walked them inside. Five bags had been left outside the door to her room.

"We picked up some supplies for you that I thought you might need while you're here. If there's anything else you need, please do let us know and we'll get them for you. In the meantime, Simon is going to be stationed outside of your room. If you need to go anywhere, he'll go with you."

Rachel glanced at the fresh-faced young man who had brought them food earlier. He looked right out of high school. She nodded in greeting.

"I'll be down at eight tomorrow morning to get you for breakfast," Jack continued.

Rachel nodded again, suddenly feeling halfway in shock about what had happened. Reality was setting in.

"Thank you for everything, Jack. I appreciate it." She grabbed a bag. "I'm sure we'll be just fine tonight."

His eyes remained on her a minute longer before he stepped back. "Good night then. I'll see you in the morning. Good night, Aidan."

Aidan grinned also. "Good night, Mr. Jack."

Rachel stepped into her room, dragging the bags with her. She crossed the sitting area to retrieve her purse and paused. What felt wrong about this room?

She looked around. Everything appeared to be in place. Really, her only belonging was her purse. She spotted it on her bed, just where she'd left it. She eyed it for a moment, looking at the lay of the straps.

That's not how she left her purse. It had been upright when she left it there.

It just fell over, Rachel.

Of course it had just fallen over. What did she think? That someone had been in her room, ruffling through her things? That would be ridiculous.

She picked up her purse to retrieve a pen. Her gut clenched. She still had the feeling that something was not as she left it, and she hoped it was simply paranoia. But what if it wasn't?

Jack rapped on Rachel's door promptly at eight the next morning. He hadn't slept all night. Instead, he'd analyzed lists and names and tried to come up with something that would give them a clue as to who was behind these attacks.

They'd come up with nothing.

Rachel opened the door looking bright eyed and surprisingly well rested. Her eyes gave her away, however. Jack could see the worry in the crinkles at their corners, see the weariness in her gaze.

"Good morning." He handed her a cup of coffee, one that he'd been tempted to drink himself.

"Coffee. How'd you know I was just wanting some of this?"

"Good guess." He nodded toward the distance. "You want to get some breakfast downstairs?"

"I'm starving—and desperate for something to do other than think."

Jack couldn't help but smile at the cadence of her words. At least she was keeping herself fairly upbeat. A moment later, she and Aidan joined him in the hallway.

"Any updates?" Rachel took a sip of her coffee as they meandered toward the mess hall.

"No updates. Right now we're looking into your friend George Anderson. He's our best lead so far."

"I'd hardly call George my friend. There was always something about him that made me keep him at arm's distance. I'm not sure if it was simply that our personalities don't connect or if he's just a little…what's the word?"

"Scary?"

She smiled. "I was going to say 'different.'"

"No one has seen him since yesterday morning."

Her head turned sharply toward him. "Really? George?"

"Really. We've got men looking for him. I'm not saying he's guilty. I'm just saying he's a person of interest."

"Wow. That's all I can say." She shook her head.

"Did the two of you ever date?" He told himself he was just asking as part of the investigation. But was he?

"George? No. Definitely not. I think he was interested, but I wasn't. I don't have time to date and, even if I did, I wouldn't date a military man. I did that once already, and now I'm a single mom."

Her words did something strange to him. Why did he feel a bit disappointed or saddened by her proclamation? He was content being single and running Eyes. Besides, he'd tried marriage once, too, and failed miserably at it. He never wanted to make that mistake again.

They went through a cafeteria-style line and picked out their breakfast choices before sitting at a table by the window. Just as they dug into their food, Denton, the assistant director for Eyes, appeared at his side. He looked serious, and Jack braced himself for whatever he had to say.

Denton looked at Rachel. "The office for Operation 26 Letters just exploded. The FBI needs to talk to you."

SIX

Rachel rushed to her feet. "My office? Was anyone hurt?"

Denton shook his head. "No, there was no one there when the bomb went off. The building is destroyed, though."

Rachel glanced at her watch. Ten. She usually got to work at 9:30 a.m. after she dropped Aidan off at preschool. If she hadn't been here at Eyes, she would have been sitting at her desk, most likely checking her emails and drinking coffee, precisely when the building exploded.

She would have been...killed.

She shuddered at the thought. Jack stood and placed a hand under her elbow, as if he feared she might pass out. She leaned into his strength for a moment, relishing having someone there to hold her up.

"They're trying to dig through your things to find anything that's usable—files, computers, etc.," Denton said, shifting his weight. He looked at Jack. "How do you want to handle this?"

"Rachel would be the best one to help extract any files that might be useful. I want the entire perimeter around the office building secured, though. By my men, not just the FBI."

"I'm on it."

Rachel looked up at Jack as Denton retreated.

"Are you okay?" Jack asked.

She nodded, still feeling dazed. She pictured her office

in flames. All of her files, her pictures, her notes. Her heart thudded with sadness.

"I'm fine. I guess." She shook her head as she tried to comprehend this new twist. "Have all of these deaths been because of my nonprofit?"

Jack flexed his jaw. "It's anyone's guess at this point. But it's more critical now than ever that we find out if the other people on the list had any connection with Operation 26 Letters. We can check with their family members, but it would be helpful if you could search through your files also…what's left of your files, at least."

She sucked in a breath. "The letter they received yesterday at the Department of Defense. It said that they weren't done yet. How long is this going to go on? Are they just trying to terrorize me? Because it's working. Maybe they're just trying to scare me to death instead of putting a—" she glanced at Aidan before lowering her voice "—a bullet through my head."

"They're trying to send a message, that's for sure. We need to figure out why you're the one they're playing games with."

"I don't know if I'm the lucky one or just the opposite."

His hand went to her back. "Come on. We need to get you to the site."

"What about Aidan?"

"We have a child-care area where you can leave him, if you're comfortable with that."

"It seems safer than bringing him with me. Besides, he might enjoy being around some kids his age."

Jack led them down the hallway to the child-care area. Though Jack had insisted that Aidan was in good hands with Olivia, the child-care director, Rachel wasn't sure whom she could trust anymore. She took him to the play-room and, though Aidan took instantly to all of the colorful toys and equipment there, Rachel couldn't seem to make her feet budge from their position at the door. How did she know who was trustworthy in a situation like this?

Jack turned to her. "I've known Olivia for more than a decade. Her son was killed fighting over in Iraq. I promise you that Aidan will be taken care of and that you have nothing to worry about."

After hearing about her loss, Rachel instantly felt a bond with the woman and stepped away from the door. She watched as Aidan went across the room and sat in Olivia's lap as if he'd known her forever. If one didn't know better, one might think the two were grandmother and grandson.

She so wished her parents were alive to spoil Aidan like every good grandparent did. She still felt the void in her life from their deaths. She'd long ago stopped asking why life wasn't fair, though. She'd simply come to the conclusion that despite life not being fair, God was still good.

But now her son was in danger...

She shook her head as she walked down the hallway. God was still good. Circumstances didn't change that. She had to cling to that knowledge even when her emotions tried to tell her otherwise.

"My car is waiting downstairs. Are you ready for this?" Jack asked.

"Ready as I'll ever be."

Once they were cruising down the road, Rachel sighed and leaned against the headrest. Her thoughts couldn't seem to settle anywhere. Instead they bounced around in her mind until a headache began to develop.

"Will this be on the news, Jack?"

"Most likely the media has heard about it."

"That's what I figured also. I'm going to need to call Nancy, the president of the Board of Directors for Operation 26 Letters. If she hears about our office on the news before she hears it from me, she's going to flip out with worry. Plus, if she's not able to contact me she's going to head to the police station and file a missing person's report. No need to put her through all of that worry."

Jack pulled the phone from his belt. "Here you go."

Rachel dialed Nancy's number, but she didn't pick up. Maybe Nancy had already heard the news and was down at the office talking with the FBI. Or maybe Nancy didn't answer because she didn't recognize Jack's phone number. Rachel had been guilty of doing that a time or two herself.

She left Nancy a vague message to call her back at Jack's number and then handed the phone back to Jack.

"Did you have a database of volunteers at the office, Rachel?"

She sucked in a deep breath. "I keep my volunteer records in one of my filing cabinets. If we can recover my hard drive, I kept a copy there, also. But, Jack, there were volunteers that I didn't have any information on. There were schools and churches and clubs where the members pulled together to send letters to military personnel overseas as a part of a one-time campaign. Other volunteers became more of pen pals and consistently wrote one or more sailors or soldiers or marines. It would be impossible to keep track of everyone who volunteered."

"It's something worth exploring."

"I agree." She rolled her head back, trying to get the kinks out of her neck, before sighing. "I just don't understand how people could be this…this evil. I always want to believe the best in people, to believe that people at their core are good."

"Keep believing that."

Her face jerked toward his. "How can you say that after everything you've seen? I mean, I think I've seen some terrible sides of humanity through this, but I'm sure what you've seen is even worse."

"I'd be lying if I said there weren't evil people out there.

But life is so much better when you believe the best in people. It's a trait I wished I possessed sometimes."

The streets faded from back roads to familiar streets that Rachel traveled—or used to travel—every day. As they turned down the street to where her office was located, she braced herself for what she was about to encounter—more evidence that someone was bent on terrorizing her.

She prayed that God would give her the strength to face this newest obstacle.

Jack stood beside Rachel in the grassy area outside of the charred remains of her office building. He stood on guard, ready to catch her if she stumbled. The way she stared at the shell of her office building, blinking rapidly as if in a daze, worried him. He was afraid her knees might buckle at any time.

"Rachel?" He touched her elbow to get her attention.

"I need to know more." Rachel continued staring at the remains of the office, not turning to speak to him. "How did this bomb get into the building? How did it detonate? Was it homemade? Military-grade?"

Jack shifted as he thought about how to best answer her questions. "Let me ask you this first: When were you in the building last?"

"When I left Friday evening after work. I didn't go in all weekend."

"That's what I figured. That means that the bomb was most likely planted in the office sometime after you left on Friday. The FBI thinks there was a timer set on it so the bomb would explode at nine-thirty this morning. Is there anything significant about nine-thirty?"

"You can always count on me to be at my desk starting my day here at nine-thirty weekdays. Like clockwork." The way she said the last word, it almost sounded as if she blamed herself for being predictable.

"Do you need to sit down? You're looking a little ashen."

Rachel didn't answer. Instead, her gaze roamed the scene. "I'm going to need to tell the board members. With all the media I see out here now, I'm sure this story has already hit the airwaves in time for the noon broadcasts. I'd hate for them to find out that way instead of from me."

"You just need to worry about yourself and your son right now. We'll have someone else contact the board. You have enough to worry about without adding that pressure to yourself."

"What about the volunteer files?"

"It doesn't look as though anything survived the explosion. The FBI has your computer, though. They'll have their best people on it, trying to retrieve your hard drive."

Her head swiveled toward him, her eyes lit with realization. "I did have some type of computer backup that... well, George, of all people, encouraged me to get a couple of months ago. It's some kind of subscription where my files are backed up to a website each evening in case my computer ever crashed. I bet that database is on there somewhere."

"We'll have someone look into it. Maybe we can find some clues in those files."

She glanced at his phone, worry stretching over her face again. "Nancy hasn't called back, has she? She's usually glued to her cell phone. I can't believe she hasn't called yet."

"She's the president of the board, right?"

Rachel nodded. "I'm sure if she saw this on the news, she would have rushed right over."

"Maybe she's on her way right now."

Rachel crossed her arms over her chest, her face pale. Jack had the urge to put an arm around her shoulders and try to comfort her, but he knew that would be crossing the line. He'd been hired to protect her and nothing more.

The FBI agent in charge approached them. He led them to a makeshift office in the back of a van. For the next hour, they questioned Rachel about who had keys to the building, who had last been inside, if she had any enemies. Jack could see the exhaustion deepen on her face with each question.

Midway through the interview, another FBI agent knocked on the van door and stepped inside. "Sir, we have another case that may be related to this one. There's a woman who was just found dead in her home. She's believed to be affiliated with this office. Her name is Nancy Clark."

Rachel gasped, her hand flying over her mouth. "No. Not Nancy. Not Nancy." A guttural cry escaped from her.

Jack broke his rule and placed his arm around Rachel's shoulders as tears began pouring down her cheeks. His heart ached at her pain, yet he felt so helpless to do anything about it. So instead, he prayed.

SEVEN

Rachel felt as though the whole place was spinning. She was almost willing just to let the turns suck her into their vortex, to mentally leave behind everything that she was trying to comprehend at the moment. Jack grasped her arm, his strong fingers encircling her biceps.

"Somebody get her some water," Jack muttered. The agent beside him pulled a bottle from a cooler in the corner. Jack opened it and handed the bottle to Rachel. "Take a drink. You keep going pale, like you're going to pass out."

"Was Nancy killed because of me?"

Jack shook her shoulders until she looked him in the eye. "None of this is because of you, Rachel. None of it is your fault. All of the blame for this falls on Apaka."

"Why do I feel guilty then? Why do I feel like it should have been me instead of Nancy? Or that I should have been in the building this morning and none of this would have happened? Are they going to keep killing people close to me to send some type of message?"

"That's what they want you to think. They want you to feel bad, to feel scared. Don't let them win, Rachel. You've got to hang in, to stay strong. Try to keep your head clear for us. That's your best retaliation at this point."

She raised her head, a new determination in her eyes. "You're right. George is missing. He knows Nancy. He has the keys to the building. I'd say he should be your number-one suspect."

Jack glanced at the agent beside him, who nodded and jotted down some more notes. "We're done. I need to get Rachel back to somewhere safe. I think she's had enough for today, but if you have any more questions, you have my cell phone number. Feel free to call." Jack turned back to Rachel. "We need to get back to Eyes. Your uncle is going to be there soon and I know he wants to see you, to make sure you're okay. That will especially be true once he hears about what happened today."

Rachel nodded, ready to get back to Eyes. She took one more glance back at the building where she'd spent so much time, energy and passion. It was hard to believe all of that was gone. That Nancy was gone.

Poor Nancy...

Jack helped her into the SUV and the vehicle hummed as Jack cranked the engine. A moment later, they were rolling down the road silently. Thoughts from the day turned over in her mind again and again, haunting her. Nancy had been one of the nicest people in the world. Her father had been in the military, and then later her own son had joined. She'd been so proud of him.

Now she was dead.

Rachel simply wanted to talk about something—anything—to get her mind off Nancy and everything else that had happened. She glanced over at Jack. She'd felt his gaze on her, assessing her as he often did. She wanted to know more about this man who'd been hired to protect her.

"Tell me about your family, Jack. Do they live around here?"

Jack offered a quick side glance at her, as if the question surprised him. "My parents live in Ohio. Dad was a teacher, and Mom stayed home with me and my brothers until we went to school. Then she went back to work as a nurse."

"Brothers?"

"Two. One older and one younger."

"Do they live around here?"

"No, one's in Indiana and the other in Maryland."

"You see your family a lot?"

"Not as much as I would like."

"You should," Rachel said. Her parents' images flashed into her mind. "One day, they might not be around and you'll wish they were."

"You're speaking from experience?"

She shrugged. "I guess you could say that. I mean, I was always close to my parents, but I had other things going on in my life. I should have given them more of my time. I thought I'd have more of it. More holidays to spend with them, more birthdays to share. You just never think their time is going to end so soon."

"I'm sure that's true. I am overdue to visit to my family. I'll have to remedy that as soon as…"

"As soon as I'm safe again? It might be a while. Maybe your parents would be better off visiting you." She'd tried to sound lighthearted but failed miserably.

Jack glanced over at her. What was that look in his eyes? Compassion? Sorrow? Anger?

She shrugged. "I am trying to look on the bright side, believe it or not. I'm still alive, aren't I?"

"We're going to keep it that way."

"I appreciate you looking on the bright side also. You don't have to pretend with me, though. I know the staggering reality of this situation."

Jack looked at her, his blue eyes intense. "Ms. Reynolds, I'm very good at my job. I won't let anything happen to you. I'd stake my life on it."

Rachel felt her cheeks flush until she looked away. Why did she believe him? She'd learned long ago not to believe impossible promises. Something about Jack seemed different, though. She wanted to believe him, and that desire was a milestone in itself.

She swallowed, her throat aching, her head still pounding. Every time she stopped talking, she started picturing Nancy, her office building, the scene at the playground yesterday. She needed to keep the conversation going if she wanted to keep her sanity.

"Ms. Reynolds?" Rachel questioned.

Jack glanced at her again, confusion in his gaze. "Pardon?"

"You just called me Ms. Reynolds. Why?"

"You're my client."

"You've been calling me Rachel all day, though."

"Which do you prefer then?"

"Rachel. Definitely Rachel." Silence fell again. Her thoughts wondered to Eyes, to the two men who were constantly at Jack's side. There was Luke, the blond-haired, fair-skinned man who seemed all business. Then there was dark-haired, bronzed Denton, who often had a toothpick in his mouth and who had tattoos peeking out from underneath his shirtsleeves. The brains and the bronze, Rachel supposed. Jack seemed like a good mix of both.

She cleared her throat. "I guess Luke and Denton are your right- and left-hand men. They seem to be wherever you are."

"Yeah, I trust them like they were my brothers. I met Denton through my work at the CIA. Luke came highly recommended by your uncle, actually. His resume was incredible, so I couldn't argue."

"It's good to have men you can trust."

"Essential."

Silence fell again. She began thinking of the excitement of the past twenty-four hours—excitement was putting it nicely.

Her life had been so routine for so long now. She'd been scheduled, organized, somewhat of a control freak. And now everything had been turned upside down.

"I used to like adventure, you know. River rafting, rock climbing, bungee jumping. I'm not saying I was successful at any of those things. But I liked trying. I liked not letting my fears hold me back. I even spent a year after college exploring Europe. I really never saw myself settling down and staying in one place."

"It sounds as though you were the perfect woman for a Navy SEAL to marry then."

Rachel's smile faded. "Maybe I was. Maybe then. Not anymore. Being a mom changes everything. And this isn't the kind of adventure I ever wanted. Even when I was adventurous, I wanted safe adventures. Adventures where I had the adrenaline rush but still knew I also had a safety net. I don't have that now."

She glanced at her hands. What she wouldn't give to have that safety net now.

I'm your safety net. You can fall back on me. Isn't that why Jack stayed so close today? Not only for her protection, but to catch her in case she fell?

That's what Jack wanted to say. But he didn't.

She'd already stumped him once by calling him out on the "Ms. Reynolds" comment. He knew the truth. He'd felt himself feeling too close to Rachel, and using the name "Ms. Reynolds" helped him put some distance between them. If he was smart, he would always call her "Ms. Reynolds." It was too easy to want to take her into his arms as it was. Anything he could do to put an imaginary wall up would be advisable, he realized.

He sensed that Rachel wanted to keep talking, so he cleared his throat. "Tell me about Andrew. How did you meet?" The best way to get his mind off of Rachel would be to talk about her husband, he supposed.

"Andrew?" She seemed to snap away from some other deep thoughts. She visibly relaxed at the mention of his name. "I was working public relations for a nonprofit and decided to participate in an ocean swim for charity that we were sponsoring. I should have known better than to try to swim five miles when I hadn't done anything of that sort since swim team in high school."

"Swim team, huh?"

She rolled her eyes. "My parents made me pick a sport, and that seemed like the easiest one at the time. Anyway, as I was swimming, a rip current caught me. Andrew saw me being pulled under and saved me. It was love at first sight."

Jack already knew part of the story from the time he spent with Andrew, but he wanted to keep Rachel talking. Plus, he was interested to hear her tell the story also. "Did you get married quickly?"

She nodded. "Andrew was leaving in four months for a six-month deployment over in Afghanistan. His SEAL team was going over to help train the military there. So, we had the choice of dating for ten months and then seeing how we felt when he returned from the Middle East. Or we could get married before he left."

"You got married before he left?"

"Yep. Two months before he left, actually." Her smile turned into a frown. "I never thought that would be the last time I saw him."

"Are you glad you got married quickly?"

A small smile returned. "Yeah, I am. The way I see it, marriage has its challenges whether you've known the person you're marrying for two months or if you've known them for two years. I knew right away that Andrew was an incredible person. I'd do it all over again, even if I knew the outcome.

Plus, there's Aidan. Aidan has been such a wonderful gift. God has a plan. All the time. Even when we don't feel like there is a plan, there is."

"Even in this situation."

Rachel nodded. "Unbelievable right now, but yeah, even in this situation."

They pulled up to Eyes and Jack glanced at the dashboard clock. "It looks like we're right on time for your uncle."

As if on cue, they spotted a black SUV coming through the gates behind them. Vice Admiral Harris.

Jack wondered if Vice Admiral Harris had any answers yet. He prayed, for Rachel's sake, that he did.

"Your friend Nancy was found murdered this morning?" her uncle repeated. "I don't like this. Not at all."

Rachel looked over at Jack, who sat across from her in the lobby of Eyes. She was thankful that he'd decided to stay with her while her uncle was here. She found something comforting about his presence.

Jack leaned forward, precision in each motion as he looked at her uncle. "The police are investigating it now. Her death has to be connected, though. I don't believe in coincidences that big."

"I agree." Her uncle shook his head and looked off into the distance. "Between that and the building blowing up this morning, it sounds like an incredibly rough day. The important thing is that you were here, not there, when it went off. All I care about is keeping you safe. You and Aidan."

Uncle Arnold patted her knee. He was like a father to her now that her own father had passed. Uncle Arnold smiled tightly, the reality of the situation showing in the strain in the lines on his face. He was in his late fifties, but he still looked youthful, even with his white hair. The military had kept him fit, sharp.

"Yes, we have been safe here." She remembered her purse and the feeling she had that someone had gone through it. Coincidence, she told herself. Her mind was on overdrive and she was reading too much into things. She rubbed her hands against her jean shorts. "Uncle Arnold, about this note from Apaka…"

He straightened, snapping back into military mode. "The terrorist organization is just trying to threaten us."

"Trying? I'd say succeeding."

He offered a half nod. "They want Abram Titov released. They say they'll leave you alone if we release him. Not that I believe them. Your name was on the list before we captured Titov. They're just using you as a pawn now."

"Nothing makes sense, Uncle Arnold." She placed her head in her hands, rubbing her temples, that were now throbbing. "I keep trying to come to terms with things, but I can't."

"Don't try to make sense of terrorists, Rachel. They don't make sense. They operate on bringing fear to people to accomplish their own agenda. They want to make a point that no one is safe."

"Have you gotten any information from Titov yet?" Jack's voice cut into the room. "Is he talking?"

"He's not talking. He won't. He'd rather die than betray Apaka."

"Any idea where this cell is hiding out?" Jack asked. "Do you have it narrowed down yet?"

Uncle Arnold shook his head. "We have some leads we're following up on. But nothing yet. We're working as fast as we can. But we have to plan each of our steps carefully. There's no room for error."

Rachel sighed, each dead end they ran up against making her head pound even harder. "I just can't figure out why my name is on the list. I've covered every possible area of my life with Jack, and we've found no connection."

Uncle Arnold nodded and brushed some lint from his crisp pants. "The connection is there somewhere. It will be discovered with time. Apaka is bound to make a mistake, and when they do, we're going to be all over it."

Denton and Aidan came pounding down the stairs at that moment. Aidan swooped into their conversation while playing with a wooden airplane. He paused by Uncle Arnold. "Guess what, Uncle Arnold? I'm going to the zoo tomorrow, and I'm going to feed a giraffe!"

Rachel's heart sank. She'd totally forgotten about his trip to the zoo. Aidan had been looking forward to it for weeks now. "About that, honey..."

Uncle Arnold held up a hand to quiet her. "Tell me more about this trip to the zoo."

"I sold lemonade to raise money for a new exhibit at the zoo, and I won this contest. Now I get to feed the giraffes! I can't wait! It's going to be so cool. My friend says their tongues feel like gooey sandpaper."

"Gooey sandpaper, huh?" Uncle Arnold laughed. "I wouldn't know about that. It sounds like a great opportunity, though."

"Aidan worked very hard to raise money and was the top earner in the area. He did more than sell lemonade. He also solicited donations around town and even hosted a puppet show in our backyard and charged an admission fee."

"Sounds like he has some of his mother in him." Uncle Arnold smiled affectionately.

"I always want to encourage him to go after causes he believes in. I'm just sorry he's not going to be able to get his award. He was really looking forward to it."

"You should take him."

Rachel did a double-take at her uncle, sure she hadn't heard him correctly. "What was that?"

"You should take him, Rachel. You can't let this place

become a prison. Besides, it could be days—or months even—until Apaka is rounded up. You know I don't believe in letting fear hold you back. If it does, then the enemy wins."

"But isn't there a difference between fear and common sense right now? I should probably just lay low."

Her uncle shook his head. "Jack should be able to arrange the trip for you. Just use extra caution. You can't hide out here forever. That's not living at all."

"I'm not sure that's a good idea," Jack interjected. He'd been quiet for most of their visit, but now Rachel could see the concern in his eyes. It had to be a very real worry for him to contradict her uncle. "Security will be difficult in that environment."

Her uncle narrowed his eyes, suddenly becoming all business. "This is what we're paying you for. Put your best men out there. I'm confident that you'll be up for the job."

"I'm not questioning your decision, but—"

"Good, then arrange for Aidan to be able to go on his field trip. He earned it. I like to see good work rewarded."

Rachel and Jack exchanged a glance. She forced a smile at Aidan, who smiled triumphantly. Jack had less than twenty-four hours to get everything together before the field trip. And Rachel had less than twenty-four hours to try and conquer her nerves before they got the best of her.

EIGHT

After eating dinner, they walked her uncle back out to the waiting SUV that would escort him back to the Department of Defense. As they hugged goodbye, Uncle Arnold grasped her arms and locked gazes with her.

"Rachel, Jack here is the best. I know he'll take care of you. You just need to listen to him. He knows what he's doing. Can you do that?"

Rachel reluctantly nodded. The more she was around Jack, the farther away she wanted to be. It wasn't that he was unpleasant. It was simply that being around Jack caused her heart to do things it shouldn't. Being with someone like Jack wouldn't be good for her or Aidan. She needed someone with a safe career, someone she could depend on to come home every evening. Jack wasn't that man—not that he'd made any offers to the position, even.

Her uncle bent down to eye level with Aidan. "You have fun at the zoo tomorrow, okay?"

Aidan nodded with a grin and then gave his uncle a hug.

Rachel wished her uncle hadn't brought the zoo up again. She was still Aidan's mom, and she still had the chance to change her mind, if that's what she thought was best for her son. Still, Uncle Arnold thought it would be okay if they went—that Jack and his men could handle it. Was she being too paranoid? She realized this complex could become a prison if she let it. Maybe getting away would be a good thing.

They watched as her uncle pulled away. She was glad he'd come, but talking to him had made everything become all too real. This wasn't a joke or a misunderstanding or a dream.

Somehow, Rachel Reynolds, a nonprofit director, had become the target of a terrorist organization. Her office building had been bombed. Terrorists had sent her threats directly to the Department of Defense. Her friend Nancy was dead, and her colleague George was the main suspect. She shook her head.

Jack turned to them. "Listen, it's been a long day. A long couple of days, for that matter. How about we go fishing?"

"Fishing?" Aidan's eyes danced with joy at the prospect.

Rachel wished she could get that excited about life again. "Would you like that, Aidan?"

He nodded with enough energy to power the entire facility. Jack had assumed as much, because he laughed lightly.

They met downstairs a few minutes later, and Jack had three fishing poles in hand. Aidan chatted nonstop as they walked across the grass, asking questions about what kind of fish they could catch, if Jack had any worms they could use, what they would do with the fish they caught. Rachel smiled as she listened to him, all the while noting how patiently Jack answered all of his questions.

Finally, they settled on the shores of the man-made lake that was used primarily for training purposes. The water looked beautiful and peaceful, a little oasis in the middle of this craziness.

Jack explained to Aidan how to bait the hook and cast the line into the water. Aidan ate up every moment of it. Within moments, Aidan was eagerly holding onto the pole, kicking his legs on the edge of the pier and singing to himself.

"He loves this," Rachel confided to Jack.

"I'm glad. Fishing is one way to have a few moments of quiet reflection. I've always loved it."

"I wanted to thank you for letting my uncle come up today and for being such a good host. I mean, I know he hired you, so it wasn't all out of politeness, but still, it means a lot."

"I'm glad he could come."

"As I'm sure you know, Vice Admiral Harris isn't actually my uncle. He and my father were best friends, and he became like part of the family. I've always called him uncle."

"Tell me about your parents."

"They worked for the Department of Agriculture doing work for farms and foreign agricultural services. I probably told you that already when I went through the massive information dump about life, didn't it?"

Jack smiled. "You might have mentioned that. But I'm not asking about them for that reason. I'm just curious about you, about how you turned out so well. Not everyone would be handling this situation with so much grace. Your parents must have done something right."

Rachel felt herself blush and looked away. "They were great parents. They both worked a lot, yes. But in the process, they taught me about the value of working hard and earning my keep, keeping my word."

"What did they think of Andrew?"

"They liked him well enough. They thought we got married too quickly, of course. But they'd gotten married equally as quickly when they met, so they couldn't exactly argue with my decision."

He cast the line into the water again. "So, the more I talk to you, the more I realize how out of character it seems for you to have gotten married so quickly. You don't seem like the impulsive type."

"I used to like being out of my comfort zone because I

thought it made me grow strong as a person. I tried to make decisions based on my gut."

"That was all in past tense."

Rachel nodded. "Now, I just want things to be stable and safe. I want to make a good life for my son."

"It's an honorable goal."

Quiet fell for a minute. Aidan continued to drop the line and jerk it back up, not too concerned about actually catching a fish.

Rachel turned to Jack. "What do you think of the zoo tomorrow? I'm not feeling one-hundred percent about it. I know what my uncle said, but—"

"I agree. I know your uncle feels confident that we can handle it. I'm just not sure I want to put you and Aidan in that situation."

"He has been looking forward to it all summer. I hate to not let him go. But I don't want anything to happen to him. And for nothing to happen to him, I have to make sure that nothing happens to me."

"I'll tell you what. If you decide to go, I'll make sure every base is covered while you're there. I'll station my best men around the premises. We'll take every precaution possible."

"Jack?"

"Yes?"

"Thank you. For everything. I mean, I know you're not exactly doing this out of the kindness of your heart. You were hired for the job." What did she just say? She frowned. "That didn't come out right. I'm fumbling my words here."

His smile reassured her. "It's okay. I think I know what you're saying."

"I'm just trying to say thank you. I appreciate everything you've done."

How could Jack tell her that even if he wasn't getting paid to do this, that he would have volunteered to do the job? He couldn't tell her that. Rachel would ask too many questions. It was just easier if she thought they were strangers with no connections up until yesterday.

"I'm glad I can be there, Rachel."

"Mr. Jack, Mr. Jack, I think I've got something!"

Jack reached for Aidan and wrapped his fingers around the fishing pole. He instructed Aidan on how to slowly reel in the line. The line emerged from the water empty.

"Where's the bait?" Aidan asked.

"Those fish must have been hungry. But there's good news."

"What's that?"

"The fish are biting. That means you might catch something yet."

Jack baited the hook and helped Aidan cast the line again.

When Jack settled down beside Rachel again, she turned to him. "Are you sure you don't have any kids hidden somewhere? You seem like such a natural."

He chuckled. "I'm quite certain."

"Have you been married before, Jack?"

Rachel's question, for some reason, made him feel like ice water had been tossed on his face. His marriage was the one subject he didn't like to talk about. Yet, after all Rachel had been made to talk about, how could he avoid the question without making her feel like a heel?

He pulled up the line again and saw the fish had eaten the bait but still managed to get away. "I was married for a couple of years."

"What happened?"

"I...I failed her. I should have been there for her and I wasn't."

"You don't seem like the type who fails at anything."

His jaw tightened. "You only know one side of me, though."

And that was the only side she was going to know, because failure wasn't ever an option again.

Rachel wondered about Jack's reaction but didn't ask about the look of dismay that crossed his features. His marriage was obviously something that he didn't want to talk about.

She bit her lip, stopping anymore questions from pouring out.

She was hardly an expert on marriage, since most of her short one had been spent apart from her husband. But Rachel truly couldn't imagine Jack failing at anything. He just seemed like the type who would have been voted Most Likely to Succeed in high school.

"Mommy, Mommy, look!" Aidan shouted. At the end of his fishing line dangled a fish of some type.

"Excellent, honey!"

Jack helped him take the fish from the line. Rachel again marveled at how good Jack was with Aidan. It warmed her heart to see how Aidan had taken to him, also. Aidan wasn't the most outgoing kid, but he acted like he'd known Jack for much longer than he actually had.

As Jack helped Aidan over at a nearby deck, Denton sauntered over. He crossed his arms as he watched Aidan squealing with delight over his fish, and a grin flashed across his face.

"So Jack took you guys fishing?"

"He did. Aidan even caught one little guy, but I don't think he has the heart to keep him. If I was a betting woman, I'd bet you he's going to let him go."

"Count yourself fortunate. Jack only takes people who are close to him fishing. It's his getaway when he needs to clear his head." For some reason, his statement caused Rachel's heart to swell a little with…what was that emotion? Pride? Joy? Whatever it was, it made no sense.

"I'm sure he has a lot of pressure on him. He said a lot of the assignments here are pretty high octane."

"He does have a lot of pressure on him, but he handles it well. Lives are at stake, so there's always a cause for pressure. But he loves this work and does a great job at it."

She cleared her throat. "Did you come out here with an update, by chance?"

"I did. I wanted to let you know that your friend Nancy was shot in the back. Most likely, she didn't even know what was coming. There were no defensive wounds or anything to indicate she put up a fight. The shot came from outside the window."

"Outside the window? Like a sniper almost?"

He nodded. "Like a sniper."

"Has anyone found George Anderson?"

"He appears to have disappeared off the face of the earth. We'll find him eventually, though. Don't give up hope."

"I haven't." Rachel's gaze scanned the trees, almost as if she expected to see George there, his face camouflaged with paint.

That was a crazy thought, though. Why would George be hiding in the trees?

Rachel knew the answer. He'd been a sniper in the military.

NINE

A farmer, a professor, a scientist.

Rachel's mind tried to connect the dots as she blew her hair dry the next morning. Nothing made sense.

An entomologist, an engineer and a nonprofit director.

Could it be a college that connected them? A birth date? Did they all visit the same website? What could they possible have in common?

She sighed and put the blow dryer down. Today was Aidan's field trip and award. Aidan smiled up at her now, beaming in his Superman shirt. This field trip was all he could talk about last night.

A crisp knock sounded at the door. It was time to go.

Rachel looked down at her son and ruffled his hair. "You ready?"

He nodded.

The question was—was Rachel ready? Not really. But if she had to spend her whole life here, she might as well just be dead. They had to get out eventually. Jack had assured her that every precaution possible would be taken.

Rachel hesitated a moment before turning the door handle. She continually second-guessed herself about the wisdom of doing this.

Jack waited on the other side of the door, his customary slacks and button-up shirt with the sleeves rolled to the elbows, gone. Instead, he wore shorts, sneakers and a T-shirt. He looked much more human in the outfit and less G.I. Joe. Still, his eyes held that serious, focused look that Rachel had become accustomed to.

"Everyone's ready," Jack said.

Rachel nodded and took Aidan's hand. "Let's go then."

A line of SUVs waited outside, and Jack shuffled them inside one. Denton sat on one side of Rachel and Aidan, while Jack sat on the other.

"Why the convoy?" Rachel asked.

"We want to make sure if Apaka knows you're leaving today, that they don't know which SUV you're leaving in. We already had another convoy leave fifteen minutes ago." He paused. "With everything that happened yesterday, we're not taking any chances."

Rachel tried to swallow, but her throat was dry. Aidan talked on and on about the trip, oblivious to the tension in the air as they pulled out of the gates. Rachel tried to listen to him, tried to nod and smile. But her gaze was drawn to their surroundings. Her thoughts hovered on Nancy, on the destruction of her nonprofit's office.

She waited, holding her breath, to see if a gunshot would splinter the glass behind them, or if flames would explode nearby.

Instead, they rolled forward, going down the road. The SUVs in their convoy slowly split apart. She knew why. If someone were following them, they wouldn't know which SUV to follow. Hopefully they'd pick the wrong one.

Rachel glanced behind them, out of the tinted rear window. From the distance, she saw a red car approaching. She watched as the vehicle came closer and closer.

Jack squeezed her shoulder. "Relax. We're okay."

Again, she tried to swallow but couldn't. Instead, she attempted a nod. The red car passed them and Rachel spotted a mother with two toddlers inside. She wanted to laugh. She'd been scared over a woman who probably lived a life very similar to hers. The driver had been oblivious to anything happening in the SUV, carrying on with what was probably a normal morning activity.

Jack leaned toward her and said in a low voice, "Agents are covering the park. You won't see them or recognize most of them because they're dressed just like us. But they're watching everything. The zoo has been informed about what's happening. Everyone will be on full alert."

Rachel nodded, but she could feel the bulletproof vest underneath her shirt. She knew that it didn't matter that safety precautions were taken. There was an inherent danger in them simply being there.

Perhaps they were putting the other children's lives at risk. What if something happened to one of them because of her? Maybe they should just go back to headquarters and for the good of everyone involved simply stay there for as long as it took, even if that meant years.

"It's going to be fine," Jack said. Why did he always seem to know her thoughts before she expressed them? Was she that transparent?

Before the zoo, they stopped at a restaurant. Jack got in the driver's seat and Denton climbed into an awaiting vehicle. The remaining five minutes it took to get to the zoo were silent, except for Aidan. Rachel tried to keep her thoughts positive. It seemed an impossible task.

At the zoo, they found a parking space. Rachel held tight to Aidan's hand as they crossed the parking lot. She walked with baited breath, half expecting to feel a bullet whiz by. Instead, she heard children's laughter, the sound of the wind brushing across the maple trees in the parking lot, the splash of fountains in the distance.

Aidan's teacher, Patricia, smiled when she spotted Aidan

and Rachel. Aidan ran to greet her with a hug before skipping on to join his classmates in line by the entrance. Rachel's gaze remained on him except for an occasional glance at Patricia.

"I'm so glad Aidan could make it. I know it means a lot to him." Patricia's gaze traveled to Jack, and her eyes glinted with curiosity. "And who is this?"

Rachel looked up, her tongue suddenly tied. How did she explain Jack? She'd been so preoccupied with Aidan's safety that she hadn't even thought that far ahead. Before she could even butcher some type of response, Jack's arm went around her waist. He reached forward with his other arm. "I'm Jack. Nice to meet you."

Patricia's eyebrows shrugged. "Lovely to meet you also. You've got yourself a good one here. We all just think the world of Rachel."

Rachel's tongue felt like sandpaper. She wanted to reject Patricia's idea that they were together. But what could she say? That Jack was the CEO and founder of Iron, Inc., and he'd been hired to protect her? That wouldn't exactly be the best route to keeping this whole thing under wraps. Besides, the area where Jack's hand met her waist seemed to be firing neurons that she didn't even know she had, making it hard to think clearly.

Jack grinned beside her. "You all think correct. Rachel's great."

Rachel's cheeks flushed. What was going on? Why was she suddenly clamming up, losing her words? All because Jack was pretending to be her date?

Patricia winked at her before hurrying back to the kids. "I know Aidan's glad you could all make it. This is going to be a great day!"

Rachel could only hope.

Rachel found Aidan in line, talking happily with his

friends. She looked back up at Jack, whose closeness was doing nothing for her nerves. "They think you're my date."

She couldn't see what his eyes were doing beneath what must be agent-issued sunglasses. "Let them think what they want to. What would you rather them think? That I'm your bodyguard?"

A date did make the most sense. And she was a grown woman. She was allowed to bring dates with her. Still, the idea seemed so foreign to her.

"They're going in." Jack offered her his hand. She stared at it a moment. "I don't bite. I promise."

She laughed airily. "I know." Hesitantly, she reached forward. His strong fingers gripped hers and suddenly her legs felt like jelly. Despite that, she followed the class through the gates and into the zoo.

Her gaze shot around the benches at the zoo entrance, looking for agents stationed around the perimeters. She spotted couples sitting together, a maintenance man picking up trash, someone lugging a cart of weeds from the garden area. Were any of them agents?

She couldn't get rid of the knots that went down her back and across her shoulders. What happens when you're out of your comfort zone? You grow. That's what she used to tell herself, at least, and that's why she had pushed herself to constantly try new adventures. She was going to have to think of this as an adventure, one where she'd come out stronger.

Right now, she was just praying that she'd come out of it at all, though.

They reached the petting zoo area, and Aidan rushed over to touch one of the goats. Rachel and Jack hung back with some of the other parents who'd come today. Rachel felt more tightly wound than a jack-in-the-box. She was quite sure that if Jack hadn't insisted on holding one of her hands, she would be wringing both of them together with anxiety.

He leaned toward her, his breath brushing her hair. "Are you okay?"

She nodded, her eyes never leaving her son. "Aside from feeling like I could pass out from anxiety, I'm doing fine."

He squeezed her hand. "You're doing great. Aidan's having fun. And we have eyes on this entire park. At the first sign of danger, we'll be on alert and you'll be whisked away."

"What about the kids? Am I putting them in danger by being here?"

"Apaka won't hurt the kids. They only want to hurt you."

Her gaze remained focused on Aidan. He squealed in delight as a goat gobbled some pellets of food from his hand. She smiled, but only for a moment.

"He's a good kid, Rachel. You've done a great job with him."

Rachel glanced up at Jack in surprise. "Thank you. That means a lot. I worry about him more than I probably should."

"I'm sure being a single parent hasn't been easy."

She shook her head, her throat burning. "No, I just do the best with it that I can." Rachel noticed him staring in the distance. "What?"

He remained silent a moment before lifting his collar and whispering something into it. Of course he'd worn a wire. It had just been carefully disguised, just like everything else about the day.

"What?" Rachel repeated.

"There's someone acting suspicious over by the Africa exhibit. Denton is keeping an eye on the situation."

Rachel tensed. "Maybe I should get Aidan. Leave." That's all she wanted to do. Grab her son and get out of here. Her gaze shot through the crowd, looking for signs of danger.

"Calm down. It could be nothing."

"Calm down? That's easy for you to say."

"No, it's not." His serious eyes cut through her. "The minute I think you're in danger, we're out of here."

He paused again, as if listening to someone in his earpiece. Rachel felt like she might come out of her skin as she waited to hear what was going on.

"It was nothing. Just a photographer setting up a photo op. Everything's fine."

"You say that a lot."

"Then we have something in common."

"What do you mean?"

"Every time I ask you how you're doing, you say you're fine, even when you're obviously not."

She didn't say anything. Jack was right. She automatically went on autopilot whenever she was asked how she was doing. She kept her real emotions bottled up all too often as she tried to remain in control.

The only problem right now was that she was in a situation where she had absolutely no control. Her only choice was to rely on God…and Jack Sergeant.

TEN

Jack had to admit that he kind of liked the feeling of Rachel's fingers intertwined with his own. And he'd be amiss if he didn't take some delight in the way she blushed at the mere hint that they were a couple. Something about being side by side with her, strolling through the zoo and keeping an eye on Aidan just felt right.

She'd made it clear that she never wanted to be with someone with his job description, though. So he didn't know why he was enjoying himself so much, especially when he knew they could never be together. Even if Rachel didn't have the convictions that she did, Jack knew there was no place in his life for a relationship. So why was it so tempting to toy with the thought whenever Rachel was around?

He looked across the way as Aidan squealed with delight at the prairie dog exhibit. "He really loves animals, doesn't he?"

"Animals and superheroes." Rachel smiled. "He's all boy. I'm always a little nervous that I'm not going to be able to help develop those boyish qualities in him. I can't exactly teach him to play baseball or how to be tough or to think like a man."

"Your uncle doesn't ever come down?"

"Not very often. Busy with his job, you know."

"I do know about busy jobs."

Silence fell for a moment. Rachel cleared her throat. "Any news on George Anderson?"

"We have witnesses that place him at work at the time the shooting in the park occurred. But that doesn't mean he's not involved. We're still investigating him."

"How about Nancy? Do they have any idea who shot her? How's her family doing? Have all of my board members been contacted?"

"Whoa. One question at a time. The FBI is handling Nancy's death, and, last I heard, they don't have any leads. I'm not sure how her family is doing. I had Luke contact everyone on the board and inform them that you've been taken somewhere safe after your office exploded. They all seemed to understand, especially given the circumstances. We also warned them all to be careful."

"What about the backup of my computer files? Were you able to access them?"

"There's someone at the office working on that now. Right now, the apparent connection of the people on this hit list is Operation 26 Letters, though we don't know why."

The group began to walk toward the Africa exhibit where Aidan would get his award. Jack scanned the crowds, just as he'd done every five minutes since they've been at the zoo. Everything appeared peaceful, like a normal day at the Virginia Zoo. But the most peaceful moments could be deceptive.

"You look worried," Rachel whispered.

"Not worried. Just alert."

The teacher looked back at them, and Jack pulled Rachel closer.

"Is that really necessary?" Rachel's voice held an edge of agitation.

Was it necessary? A good question, but why miss an opportunity? "Look happy, so no one gets suspicious," Jack said.

A smile crossed her features. Jack could tell she tried to

soften the tight lines at her lips, but it didn't work. Her smile looked forced. And he was pretty sure she was blushing again.

"Ms. Reynolds?"

Rachel's head swung toward the voice. Jack looked up and saw a woman with a cameraman trailing her. She thrust a microphone in Rachel's face. Rachel raised a hand to shield herself from the lens just as Jack stepped between them.

"I'm Vanessa Rodgers with Channel 8. We'd agreed to do a Top Kid of the Week special on your son, Aidan, and his award here at the zoo today."

Rachel's shoulders sagged and she frowned. "I'd totally forgotten. Listen, I'm sorry to do this to you, but it's not a good time. Some things have happened since then and—"

"By 'some things,' do you mean the bombing of the building housing your nonprofit, Operation 26 Letters?"

"This is not the time or place," Rachel muttered.

"Does the FBI have any leads as to who was behind the bombing?"

"No comment," Jack said. He kept Rachel moving but the reporter stayed on them.

"Is it true that it was an anti-military group behind the attack?"

"No comment," Jack repeated. "I'm going to have to ask you to leave, ma'am. This isn't the time or place to ask those questions."

"Can we set up a time somewhere else then?"

"Please, just leave," Rachel said.

Jack heard the strain in her voice.

"Is everything okay?" Patricia appeared with a worried expression on her face.

Rachel nodded. "I'd forgotten that the media was coming to this event. I'm sorry, Patricia, but this just isn't a good time, not with the bombing at my office."

Jack motioned to two of his men. They stepped forward and distracted the reporter while Jack led Rachel away. It was too late to pretend nothing had happened, though. Crowds of onlookers stared at them, including all of the children in Aidan's class.

Jack placed his hand on Rachel's back. "It's going to be okay. You did just fine."

"I can't believe I forgot about that. How could I have forgotten?"

"You've had a lot of other things on your mind, to say the least."

"And now everyone is staring." She rubbed her forehead and closed her eyes.

"They'll start minding their own business soon." His gaze scanned the crowd again for anyone suspicious. With everyone staring at them, everyone seemed suspicious.

His job just got exponentially harder.

Though Rachel was immensely proud of Aidan for his fundraising efforts, she was counting down the minutes until they could leave. Her cheeks still felt flushed from her earlier encounter with that reporter, and she self-consciously kept brushing her forehead when she noticed the looks the other parents gave her.

She'd contacted the media herself about Aidan's award. She was a former public relations spokesperson, so she had contacts within the media. She'd hoped to gain attention for the zoo and its projects. As a nonprofit director, she knew all about how important funding was for such groups.

Of course, the reporter had seemed more interested in the bombing of her nonprofit than Aidan getting his award. She frowned. Go figure.

She remembered Jack's admonition that if the media reported on the list, the terrorists would simply get the publicity they desire and spark the fear in people that they longed for. She wouldn't let that happen. That was one battle they wouldn't win, if she had anything to do with it.

But if she thought everyone believed her excuse that she just needed to get away, she was delusional. Patricia continually gave her fleeting looks, and a wrinkle of concern seemed permanently pressed between her eyes.

"Don't look so worried," Jack whispered.

Just the feel of his breath on her ear made her muscles tighten again. Why was she letting the man have this effect on her? Was she a teenager, inexperienced with the opposite sex? Hardly. But that's what she felt like.

"Mommy! Mommy! Look!" Aidan ran over and thrust his plaque into her hands.

"Congratulations, honey. I know you worked hard to earn this. I'm so proud of you."

"I get to go feed the giraffes now!"

Rachel tried to smile as he skipped away to join the zoo-keeper. She looked around, waiting to see someone out of the ordinary appear. She waited to hear gunshots, to feel a panicked frenzy spread throughout the crowd. Instead she heard children laughing, a lion roaring, a custodian pass with a squeaky cart.

From below, she saw Aidan holding a handful of hay. She held her breath, anxious for him to be beside her again. From across the deck, she spotted Luke dressed in casual clothes. A woman stood beside him and together they pointed at the animals and she pulled up a camera to snap a picture. If Rachel hadn't known who he was, she would have never guessed he was an Eyes agent.

Finally, Aidan joined her back on the viewing platform and they began the last leg of their field trip to the zoo.

Lord, You've gotten us this far. Is it too much to ask for a few more minutes?

With relief, they approached the exit. Her heartbeat finally slowed as they stepped outside the gates. Jack still kept up his façade as they left by holding her hand as they walked through the parking lot. At least, Rachel justified, she did feel safe with Jack so close. Physically, at least. Her heart was a different story. Her heart fluttered with betrayal every chance it got.

Jack lifted his collar and spoke into the wire there. Suddenly, his grip on her hand tightened. She looked up and saw his gaze darting around the parking lot. Every sense seemed to be on alert.

"What's going on?" Rachel whispered, throat tightening. She pulled Aidan closer.

"Come on. We've got to go." Jack's gentle tug on her hands became an urgent pull. In two heartbeats, he grabbed Aidan and whisked them across the parking lot. He pushed them into the SUV just as a man threw himself against the windshield and began banging on it frantically.

Rachel sucked in a breath.

It was George Anderson.

ELEVEN

"Stay down!" Jack barked.

Rachel didn't have to be told. She hugged Aidan, trying to shield him from the chaos around them.

George beat against the windshield. "Rachel! Rachel!"

Rachel tried to block out George's voice, the desperation she heard there. Had he been behind the attacks this whole time? Had he tried to kill her?

Yells sounded outside the window as Denton and Luke grabbed George off of the SUV. George flailed, slugging Luke in the mouth. Finally, Denton caught him in a choker hold, while Luke came to his senses and cuffed him.

Rachel closed her eyes and hugged Aidan even tighter. Was this it? Would George be arrested and this nightmare finally end?

"Stay put," Jack ordered, his hand on the door handle.

What choice did they have? She had no desire to go anywhere near George.

Jack climbed from the SUV and approached George. Rachel strained to make out their conversation but couldn't.

"Who was that man, Mommy? Was it Mr. George?"

Rachel's throat burned. "Yes, honey. It was."

"What's wrong with him?"

"I have no idea. Maybe Mr. Jack can tell us, though."

"Because Mr. Jack is a superhero?"

She ruffled her son's hair. "He's not really a superhero, sweetie. You know that, don't you?"

"I like him, Mommy."

She rested her chin atop his head. "I'm glad, honey." Why did hearing Aidan say that cause her heart to do strange things? Aidan was becoming attached to Jack. She could tell by the light in Aidan's eyes when he looked at Jack. Soon, hopefully, they'd be safe, and Jack would be out of their lives. Rachel had a feeling, though, that it would be a crushing blow to her son when that happened.

Jack knocked at the window and Rachel cracked the door open. No sooner had it opened when she heard George in the background. "Are you okay, Rachel? Are you hurt?"

Rachel looked at Jack, confused, desperate for answers.

Jack stepped closer to her. "He claims you were abducted."

Rachel tilted her head. "What?"

"He claims you were abducted and he was trying to save you."

"You mean, he's not working for Apaka?"

"Luke and Denton are taking him down to the FBI office for questioning, but he's claiming to be on our side."

"I see."

"And he wants to talk to you."

Rachel just wanted to go back to headquarters and hide in her room. On the other hand, maybe she needed to hear George out, find out what he'd been thinking. Finally, she nodded. "Okay. I'll talk to him."

A moment later, Denton brought a handcuffed George to the SUV. He shoved him into the front seat. "We patted him down. He's got nothing on him," Denton told Jack.

George—thirty-something, short and wiry with a shaved head that hid a receding hairline—turned toward the backseat.

Sweat covered his brow, and his gaze looked almost frantic. "Rachel, are you okay?"

"Am I okay? I'm fine. What are you doing, George? How did you know I was here? What were you planning to do?"

"Rachel, you disappeared. Your office was blown up. I knew something was wrong."

"How'd you know I was at the zoo today?"

"You told me that you'd be here today the last time I talked to you. I decided to see if you would show up. What's going on? Who are these goons?"

"They're not goons, George. They're protecting me."

"What's going on, Rachel? I know something's not right. I just want to help."

Rachel glanced over at Jack, and his look made it clear that he was leaving the decision what to share up to her. She drew in a deep breath and prayed that God would help her to find the right words. "I can't discuss it right now, George. But some very dangerous people want me dead. Those people are being tracked down right now."

"I want to help."

"You can help by just letting people believe that I'm okay. We don't want the media to catch wind of this. We just want the people behind these attacks to be captured before they can do any more harm."

His gaze fell on Jack. "Don't I know you? Afghanistan, right?"

Jack looked out the window at Denton. "Get him out of here. We've caused enough of a scene already. We need to get Rachel and Aidan to safety."

"Rachel—"

"We've got to go, George. I do appreciate the fact that you were looking out for me. Thank you for that."

"But—"

Before George could say anything else, Denton pulled him out of the SUV and slammed the door.

Rachel lay in bed, reviewing the events from the day. How could she not? She'd felt so much relief, followed by adrenaline rushes, then confusion and more paranoia.

Who would have thought that George Anderson of all people would have shown up at the zoo? That he would have remembered that she mentioned going there today for Aidan to receive his award?

Rachel thought he had good intentions—although Jack hadn't been so sure. George had always tried to keep an eye on her since Andrew died. Jack thought it was way too suspicious that George had shown up today. He'd been quiet for most of the ride home, looking even more tense than usual, if that were possible.

She remembered the look that George had given Jack before he was ushered out of the SUV. George thought he knew Jack from Afghanistan, and Rachel thought Jack looked familiar. Rachel still felt certain that Jack knew more about Andrew than he let on. Why wouldn't he tell her? It didn't make sense.

Rachel had a feeling that there was a lot about Jack Sergeant that she didn't know. Would she ever know? He wasn't the type to easily open up. He was probably the type of man who didn't like to open up—the exact type who was terrible in a relationship.

Then why did she find herself picturing what it would be like to have a future with Jack? Was it because her emotions had gotten the best of her today? When Jack had held her hand, when he'd stood close, put his arm around her waist, it had stirred up something inside her.

No, she chided herself. She was being foolish. Even if Jack were the type she was interested in, there was still the issue of his job. She didn't want to lose two husbands before she reached thirty. Then there was the small issue of his emotional closure. She couldn't even dream of a relationship with someone who wasn't willing to share his life with her. She'd only end up unhappy and miserable. Besides, exactly what had happened with his ex-wife? He'd said he screwed up. What did that mean?

She shook her head. She shouldn't even be thinking such thoughts. Instead, she listened for a moment to Aidan sleep, at the even sound of his breathing. Despite everything that had happened today, she was glad they'd gone to the zoo. Glad he'd gotten the award he'd worked so hard to achieve.

A sound perked her ears. She sat up in bed. Was that her door leading to the hallway clicking open?

She watched the light underneath her door, which was already faint at best, waiting to see if a shadow might pass by.

She held her breath, hardly wanting to breathe lest the sound interrupt her careful listening. She waited for a footfall, a creak, the turning of the doorknob.

Why would someone be in her room here at Eyes? That wouldn't make sense. She was safe here. Jack had promised her.

She remembered her purse, the feeling that someone had gone through it. Could the terrorists have breached security here? It was possible. Jack himself had said these men were brilliant, not simply cave-hoppers without a plan. They had resources, he'd said. Money. They could look like any of the men who worked here. That's what she feared the most. How they might blend in.

Her heart began racing, the rhythm pounding in her ears.

Her eyes remained on the bottom of the door.

Nothing.

She shook her head. She was just imagining things. She had to be.

Her shoulders sagged for a moment as she realized her foolishness.

Until a shadow passed beneath the door.

Someone was in the living room, she realized.

TWELVE

She grabbed her cell phone from the bedside table and held down the 1. It only rang once. Jack sounded alert when his voice came on the other line.

"Someone's in my room," Rachel whispered, her throat straining with each word.

"Rachel?"

"I don't want them to hear me."

"Stay where you are. I'm on my way."

Rachel saw the shadow move again. Subtle, like ink spreading through water.

Or was she seeing things? Were her eyes playing tricks on her? She could hardly breathe, hardly move.

Her eyes shot across the room. Was Aidan okay?

She could still hear his steady breathing and make out his small outline in bed. She breathed a short-lived sigh of relief, but they weren't out of danger yet.

Jack would be here soon. He'd help them.

But what if he didn't get here in time?

Fear scrambled across her skin. Panic sent off alarms in her head. Her lungs felt like someone pressed down on them.

Jack, get here soon. Please.

She heard another click from the other room. The light brightened under her doorway. A soft knock sounded at her door. "Rachel, it's me, Jack."

She scrambled from the bed to the door, thankful she'd worn sweats and a T-shirt to bed. She threw the door open and saw Jack's massive frame filling the doorway. Without thinking, she threw her arms around him. He seemed stunned a moment before his arms encircled her also. She found comfort for only a moment in his strong arms, his steady heartbeat.

What had she just done? Was she having crazy fantasies that their little act at the zoo today was the real deal? As quickly as she hugged him, she stepped back and straightened herself. "Sorry about that."

In the darkness, she couldn't see his expression. But she did feel his arms slip from around her and she missed them.

"It's clear. There's no one in your room."

"There was someone."

"Luke is searching the perimeters of the building now, looking for anyone suspicious. We're also looking for Simon."

"Simon? Isn't he supposed to be outside my door at all times? Did something happen to him?"

Just then, someone filled the doorway to the hall. Simon. "What's going on?" Rachel heard the uncertainty in his voice.

"Where were you?" Jack demanded.

"I just had to take a quick bathroom break. I've only been gone five minutes, max."

"It was five minutes too long, Simon. Rachel said she heard someone in her room."

His eyes widened. "That's impossible. The door is locked. I would have heard someone coming down the hall. I would have noticed something."

"We'll talk about it later." Jack looked back at Rachel. "Does anything look different to you here?"

Her gaze scanned the room. She kept most of her things in the bedroom area with her and not in the living room. She spotted some coloring books, puzzles, crayons, the letters she'd been writing for her nonprofit. Everything appeared as she'd left it. She shook her head.

"You're sure someone was in here?"

"I saw the shadows passing under the door. I heard a click." But was she sure? Why did she doubt herself so easily?

"Could the shadows have been Simon stepping away from his post perhaps?"

Rachel pulled the arms of her sweatshirt over her hands before crossing her arms over her chest. "I suppose."

She glanced back at Aidan, thankful he was sleeping so peacefully still. "Maybe I'm…maybe I'm losing it. I don't know."

Jack's hand came down on her shoulder. "Why don't you close the door so we don't disturb Aidan?"

She gently pulled the door closed, though not all the way. She still wanted to be able to hear if he woke up and needed her. Jack motioned to Simon, who stepped outside into the hallway and closed the door. Then Jack flipped on a small lamp by the couch before sitting her down.

His cell phone buzzed. He took it from the clip at his belt and mumbled a few things into the mouthpiece. Finally, he thanked Luke and snapped the phone closed.

"What is it?" Rachel sat on the edge of her seat.

"He didn't find anything or anybody."

Her shoulders sagged.

Jack sat down on the couch beside her. "Hey, chin up. That's good news."

"Or it means I'm losing my mind."

"It's normal for people in a situation like this to have heightened senses. I'd rather you be on guard than lackadaisical."

She sighed and leaned back into the couch. "What am I going to do, Jack?"

"What do you mean?" He settled back into the cushions also.

"I can't live the rest of my life like this. What if whoever is behind these attacks is never caught? When if I'm in danger for the rest of my life?"

"That's not going to happen."

"How can you be so sure?"

"Because I'm going to make sure that doesn't happen."

Their gazes caught and Rachel found herself being sucked into the deep blue of Jack Sergeant's eyes. Her heart pounded in her throat. She believed him. Again. She barely knew the man, but, for some reason, she knew she could trust him.

She also knew she had to change the subject. She was beginning to feel a bond with him that she shouldn't feel. He was out of bounds, and she needed to remember that. It was simply a matter of reminding her heart. Her head wouldn't let her forget.

She tucked her legs beneath her and tried to clear her head. She wanted desperately to forget about the situation at hand and feel halfway normal for a moment. "What do you like doing when you're not working, Jack?"

His eyes flickered toward her a moment, as if surprised. "Not working? When does that happen?"

Rachel smiled softly. "Surely you have some kind of life outside of this place."

"Eyes is my life. But if I wasn't working so much, I think I still might be somewhat of a homebody. Just staying in, eating dinner with friends, renting a movie, maybe hosting barbecues in the backyard."

Rachel smiled. "My parents used to love having barbecues. It became somewhat of a joke in our circle because they probably had one every week at least. They'd invite anybody and everybody—they called it good old Christian hospitality.

They had over coworkers from the Department of Agriculture, neighbors, childhood friends."

"Sounds like fun."

"It was. I still have all of their old picture albums. I like to look through them and remember those good times. My mom...she had a real gift for making people feel welcome. And my dad was always cracking jokes. I have pictures of myself at those cookouts from the time I was a toddler sitting on my dad's shoulders all the way up until I got married."

"Sounds like you had a great family."

"I did." She swallowed, all too aware of the hole that had been left in her life since they'd been gone. "But not everything was perfect. There's no such thing as a perfect family, right?"

"What do you mean?"

"My parents' jobs were quite stressful, especially in the days leading up to their death. They just seemed to be walking around with the weight of the world on their shoulders."

"Did they say why?"

"Only that some positions had been eliminated and now they had to finish a bigger workload within the same number of hours. Typical office stuff. They said it was nothing for me to worry about."

"I guess we all feel like that sometimes about our jobs."

"It's true."

"Did your parents like Andrew, Rachel?"

"At first." Her heart thudded as she remembered her last conversation with her parents about Andrew.

"What changed?"

Her throat burned. Should she even share? She hadn't talked about what had happened in years. She tried to forget. But did she ever really forget? No. Her suspicions always remained in her subconscious.

"I found some letters that a woman wrote Andrew." She

glanced at Jack, afraid she might see in his gaze that he felt sorry for her. Instead, she saw that he was listening, really listening. She continued. "I began fearing that he had an affair with someone. I asked him about it once. He said he would explain to me one day, that it would all make sense. Of course, he died before that could happen."

"I'm sorry, Rachel."

She nodded, trying to maintain her composure. "I tried to justify that maybe there was some other reason a woman would send him letters like that. But then, after Andrew died, I discovered that he had a separate credit card account set up and he was sending large chunks of cash advances to someone…most likely the same woman." She sighed, as the weight of her burden tugged on her. "I'm still trying to pay it off."

"Did you ever find any answers?"

She shook her head. "No, I didn't. I try not to think about it, figuring it will do me no good."

Jack leaned forward. "Rachel, I'm going to need to see those letters."

Her heart thudded. "Why?"

"Maybe they're the connection we're looking for."

Jack remembered the reason he was in Afghanistan—the suspicions that Andrew might be selling government secrets. The man would often disappear into town, unaccounted for for hours. He'd been spotted in secret, meeting with some Afghan natives. Later, they'd discovered who the true traitor was. That man, an army ranger, had been tried and convicted of treason. But what if there was some validity to the government's original allegations about Andrew? Could the letters have any connection or offer any validity to those suspicions? Jack thought he'd cleared Andrew of any wrongdoing, but what if he'd been wrong?

His heart thudded with sadness for Rachel as he saw the

anguish in her eyes. He'd wanted to pull her into his arms and try to provide some comfort. But he couldn't cross that line. Rachel was out of bounds. He couldn't let himself forget that, as he frequently seemed to do.

Looking at her earlier, at the vulnerability in her eyes, he'd wanted nothing more than to lean over and kiss her, to see if the spark that he felt sure would be there was there.

His ex-wife's, Jennifer's, image flashed in his mind. She'd once been so full of spark and life. They'd started life together full of dreams, determined to make it as a military family. They'd been young, perhaps foolish even.

Jack had been sent overseas on his first six-month deployment. He called Jennifer often. Each time, he noticed a little more of her sparkle fading. He'd moved her to a new place where she knew no one and then he'd left her. Abandoned her. She'd had a hard time making new friends. She was miserable at her job. She'd begged him to come home.

He'd only had two months until he was supposed to return. He thought she could wait it out at that point. Finally, he arrived back in Norfolk, expecting Jennifer to be excited that he was finally home. There was no one at the base to greet him when he stepped off of the ship. He'd gotten a ride home. Jennifer was inside, curled up on the couch. She barely acknowledged that he was there.

He tried to get her help. Asked her to go see a counselor or a doctor even. She said no, insisted she was fine.

Three months later, he was deployed again, this time for four months. Jennifer decided to go back to Ohio and stay with her parents for this deployment. Jack had thought it was a great idea. She needed to be around people who loved her. He knew deployment was hard, but military couples dealt with it all the time. He hoped to become a SEAL when he returned from that deployment. Doing so, he would most likely be in town for longer periods of time. It would be easier on their marriage.

But it was too late. When he returned from that deployment, Jennifer had already fallen into the arms of another man. She filed for divorce papers and refused to talk with him.

He should have seen the signs. He should have done everything within his power to stay home, to be with her. He never wanted to put someone through that again. Even though he'd become a Christian since then, the mistakes he'd made back then still haunted him.

And Rachel had made it clear that she found his lifestyle way too dangerous for him to be the family man she desired. He could understand. She wanted stability for herself and for her son. What mother wouldn't want that? It had been hard enough for Aidan to lose a father once. Rachel didn't want to put herself in a position to have him lose two male figures in his life.

He met Luke in the hallway. "Everything's clear, Jack. I checked in with the guards at the gate. No one's been in or out. I checked the videotape of the surrounding area. There's nothing suspicious."

"She feels confident that someone was in her room."

"Are you sure she's just not being paranoid?"

Jack gave him a sharp look.

"I mean, I wouldn't blame her if she was."

"Don't talk about her like that again, Luke."

"Jack, if you don't mind me saying so, are you sure you're not getting a little too close to your client? I'd hate for you to lose your objectivity."

"I'm not. And I do mind."

"I'm just trying to watch out for you, boss."

"You can watch out for me by letting me get some rest. It's been a long night."

"Yes, sir."

Jack scowled as he pushed the door open to his room. He didn't know why a heaviness had settled over him, but it had. Even worse was the urgency he felt to find the people behind the attacks on Rachel. He had a feeling they were getting impatient with waiting.

THIRTEEN

Jack watched Rachel as she sat across from him in his office the next morning. She twisted her fingers together, and her eyes had a far off look to them. Any minute now, Luke and Denton should be calling. He'd sent them over to Rachel's house to retrieve the letters.

Jack could tell by Rachel's face that she was dreading seeing the letters again, dreading the memories they would bring back.

He hated to think that Andrew could have hurt her like that. He thought he'd cleared Andrew of any suspicions, but could what he was hiding the whole time have simply been an affair?

He'd already done a search on the woman, Meredith O'Connor. Her family had worked for a mission in Afghanistan for the past twenty years. Her father had been killed four years ago.

Around the same time Andrew was in Afghanistan...

Meredith was currently living back in the United States, only a few hours away. What if Andrew had been selling secrets to Apaka? What if Meredith was a part of one of their cells? She would easily blend in, and no one would suspect.

Finally, Jack's cell phone rang.

"You're not going to like this," Denton said.

"What is it?"

"Rachel's place has been ransacked. Looks like someone just went crazy looking for something."

"We've had guards watching the place for more than a week now. How did someone get in?"

"I'm not sure how they got around our security measures. But someone's definitely been here, and it's not pretty."

"I want to talk to the men who were keeping watch. I want to find out how this happened."

"There's more."

Jack braced himself. "Okay."

"They left a message on her wall."

"What did it say?"

"It said, 'We're getting closer.'"

Jack gritted his teeth for a moment as the facts settled in his mind. "Was anything taken?"

"You'd have to ask Rachel about that. It looks like all the big stuff is still there. The TV, computer, jewelry."

He hung up and saw Rachel looking at him with questioning eyes. "What's going on?"

"Your house. It's been turned upside down."

She shivered and her hands clamped down across her chest and over her arms. "You think they were looking for me?"

"No. They were trying to send a message, to let you know that they're not backing off."

"I guess it would be crazy to think they might just disappear with time."

"I'm going to go over and take a look."

"Can I go?"

"I don't think that would be a good idea."

"Please. I need to pick up a few things. Besides, I need to see it with my own eyes."

The pleading look in her gaze made it hard to say no. "We'll have to use the utmost caution."

"Of course."

Finally, he nodded. "The FBI is headed over there now. We'll meet them there."

He placed his hand on the small of her back and led her from his office to an SUV that was waiting outside. Once she was securely inside, he ran around to the driver's side and climbed in. He noticed Rachel's white-knuckled grip on the armrest.

"You sure you want to do this? You can stay here."

"I need to go. I need to see."

They started down the road. Jack kept his gaze on alert, glancing around them for any sign of danger.

"I keep thinking that the connection of the people on the list is right at the edge of my reasoning," Rachel said. "I just can't figure out what's been nagging me."

"We've compared nearly every detail of every person's life. If I didn't know better, I'd think the names were random, but we know that's not the case. There's a reason you all were picked to be on that list."

"You still think it might have something to do with those letters?"

"We won't know until we get a hold of them."

"I'm sure you've already looked into Meredith."

What could Jack say? He knew he could only tell her the truth. "We did."

She paused a moment before quietly asking, "Was my husband having an affair with her?"

"I don't know, Rachel."

She nodded, as if accepting his answer. "Tell me about her."

"Rachel…"

"I can handle it."

Jack drew in a deep breath. "She's twenty-five years old. Her mother was from Uzbekistan and her father was an American. She grew up in New York and after college became an aid worker in the Middle East."

"Uzbekistan? Isn't that the country that Apaka is based out of?"

Jack nodded. "It is."

Rachel shook her head. "Was my husband paying off a terrorist organization? Was he involved with them somehow?" She turned to Jack. "You'd tell me if he was, wouldn't you? That connection can't be a coincidence."

"It's a possibility, Rachel. We don't know anything yet. As far as we know, Meredith and her family have no connection with Apaka."

"Isn't that what terrorists do? They blend in? They could be anyone, anywhere, hiding in plain sight within the melting pot of America."

"Remember, try not to look for the worst in people. Try to look at them and see the best. It's a gift to be able to do that."

She crossed her arms and looked out the window as they traveled toward her house. "I want to do that. I really do."

Jack reached across the seat and squeezed her knee. "I'm sorry, Rachel." It was all he knew to say as he watched Rachel's world fall further apart.

"Thank you, Jack."

Jack knew the rest of the day wasn't going to get any easier, however. Seeing her house in shambles would be just one more test. All Jack knew to do was to help hold her up if she felt like falling down. Would that be enough?

Rachel stepped over a broken vase and picked up a picture frame containing a photo of her and Aidan that lay trampled on the floor of her living room. She outlined their images with her fingertips before looking up and shaking her head. "They really did a number on this place, didn't they?"

No shelf had been unturned. Books lay scattered on the floor, picture frames were smashed and the couch had even been overturned. Then there, in streaked red letters on her dining room wall, was the message she wasn't meant to miss. *We're getting closer.*

Rachel stared at the deep red letters and turned to Jack. "Blood?"

He shook his head. "Just paint. They wanted it to look like blood, though. Makes more of an impact that way."

"I'd say." She stepped over some more of her stuff and shook her head. "When was this done?"

"We've had someone on patrol around your house since you've been at Eyes. Whoever did this must have known our schedule because they came in at just the right time. They even knew where the video cameras had been hidden."

Rachel swung her head toward him and raised an eyebrow. "Video cameras?"

"We placed them around your property just in case anyone decided to creep around here."

"How well concealed were they?"

"You had to really look for them to notice them."

"So how did they know?"

Jack's jaw flexed. "That's what we're trying to figure out."

"Did they leave any evidence?"

"The FBI hasn't found anything yet."

"It sounds like these terrorists know what they're doing. I just don't understand what they were trying to prove by doing this. Haven't they scared me enough? Why not just take me out at this point?"

Rachel looked up and saw Jack's jaw slacken as his eyes widened. Her words had surprised him. She sighed and shook her head. "Am I being too blunt?"

His game face returned. "No, you're actually too far on the right track. We're trying to put all these puzzle pieces together, to figure out the methods behind their madness.

I don't know why they keep playing games with you. But there's a reason. We just have to figure it out."

Rachel cleared a chair and plopped down. She reached down into the mess at her feet and picked up a photo album. She rubbed her fingers across the cover. How she loved pictures of her family, pictures from times past.

She opened the book and flipped through the pages. Most of them were from those famous cookouts her parents used to have. She looked at the pictures of her mom and dad smiling. Her dad holding the spatula and wearing a "Kiss the Cook" apron. Her mom proudly displaying a platter of grilled kabobs. Such memories.

The next page held a picture of Andrew with his arm around Rachel. They'd only been married a couple of weeks when that picture was taken. She remembered how happy she'd been that day as she introduced Andrew to all of her parents' friends and coworkers.

She flipped the page and saw a torn edge. Why had a page been torn out of this album? Strange.

"What is it?" Jack asked. He was always there, always observing.

"It may be nothing, but there's a page torn out of this photo album."

He leaned beside her and looked at the tear before turning to the FBI agent beside them. "Did you find a loose photo album page anywhere?"

"I'll check the evidence log, but I don't recall."

"Keep your eyes open for it."

"You think this could be significant?" Rachel asked Jack.

"Everything can be significant." Jack looked closer. "Do you remember what was on that page?"

She looked at the pages before and after again. "It would have to be more pictures from that same barbecue."

"Why would the terrorists want a picture from a family barbecue?" Jack seemed to be thinking out loud.

Rachel cleared her throat. "I think Andrew may have been in those pictures. Do you think that's why they could have been taken?"

"Your guess is as good as mine. Do you remember who else was at that barbecue?"

"Only the people I can see in these pictures. I can't even remember most of their names. Uncle Arnold was there. Me. Andrew. Mom and Dad, of course. The rest of these people were from my parents' job, I think."

"We'll try to find someone at the Department of Agriculture who can identify everyone. Maybe it will give us some kind of lead."

Rachel nodded. "Maybe."

Rachel leaned back in the chair. Why did she have the feeling that *she* was the connection on the terrorist list? The only thing she couldn't figure out was why.

FOURTEEN

Jack knew that now more than ever he had to do everything within his power to keep Rachel safe.

She looked pale as she sat beside him in the SUV, and he was almost certain she'd lost weight in the few days since coming to Eyes. Jack knew enough about Rachel to know that she was once vivacious and full of energy. She seemed to be becoming a shell.

Seeing her house ransacked and realizing that the terrorists had stolen a page from her photo album had only added to her stress.

Why would they steal pictures from her album, of all things? The question wouldn't leave his mind as he drove down the road headed back to Eyes. At least the FBI now had the letters from Meredith. Maybe they would discover something within them that would give a clue about Rachel's connection with the list. The FBI had also recovered some files from Rachel's computer at Operation 26 Letters and were searching those records now, hoping to find something— anything—that would provide some answers.

"Jack, tell me about your wife."

Jack's heart felt like it stopped for a minute. Of all the conversations he wanted to have with Rachel, this was not one of them. He glanced over at her and saw how she looked so earnest and sincere with her wide eyes.

"What do you want to know?"

Rachel shrugged. "I don't know. Start at the beginning, I suppose. How'd you meet?"

"I came home for a holiday visit my first year being enlisted," Jack started, the memories still as vivid as if it were last week. "We met at a friend's Christmas party. We started a long-distance relationship. A year later, we got married and she moved to Norfolk where I was stationed."

"How long were you married?" Rachel's gaze still held that compassionate, soft look that so easily sucked him in and made him want to forget about everything else around. Yet instead of thinking about Rachel, he had to think about his ex-wife, his past failures. Any hope he had for a future with Rachel seemed to extinguish like a candle in a windstorm.

"A year and a half."

"What happened?"

"I moved her away from everyone she knew to a place where she knew no one. And then I went out to sea for eight months."

"Did she get a job? Join a church? Find a support group for military wives?"

Jack shook his head. "No, I wasn't a Christian back then, and we didn't go to church anywhere. I kept encouraging her to get a job or do something to get out of the house. She just didn't seem interested. She always had excuses. At first, she said she wanted to get moved in and adjusted to being in Virginia. Then she said she couldn't find a job that she liked. She couldn't relate to any of the other women in the military wives' support group. She missed her family and friends in Ohio terribly."

"It sounds like she didn't make much effort to adjust to life here."

"I should have seen what was coming."

Rachel leaned toward him. "Seen what?"

He shook his head as the memories flooded him. "I should have known that she was sinking into depression. I should have seen the signs. I should have done everything within my power to get off the ship I was stationed on and get home. I could have helped her."

"What happened, Jack?"

The muscles in his neck flexed as his throat tightened. "I came home from my deployment. Needless to say, she wasn't at the base to greet me. She barely even looked up when I walked into the house. She was sitting curled up on the couch wearing her pajamas and a bathrobe. The house was a wreck. Bills had been left unpaid."

"I'm sure it was hard to see her like that."

"Hard would be an understatement. She was vibrant at one time. The life of the party. I'd underestimated how poorly she was doing while I was overseas. I thought maybe she was exaggerating, but when I saw her, I knew she wasn't."

"Did you get her help?"

"I tried to, but she wouldn't see a counselor. I was home for four months. She really seemed to start doing better. We went out every weekend with my friends and their spouses. She finally found a job working as a teacher's aide at a local elementary school. I felt like there was hope for my marriage again."

It was the first time he'd really talked about this in years. His divorce had been finalized nearly ten years ago. Yet he still struggled with the memories, the demons from his past.

"Hope is always good."

"Unfortunately, I had to go back out to sea. She decided she was going to stay with her parents in Ohio for this deployment so she didn't fall back into the same habits and thoughts. I thought it seemed like a good idea. But she never came back to Virginia. She fell in love with someone else while she was in Ohio and filed for divorce. As soon as it was finalized, she married this other guy. She wouldn't even talk to me. Once she'd decided it was over, there was no changing her mind."

Rachel grabbed his hand. "I'm so sorry, Jack. I can't imagine how difficult that must have been for you."

"I begged her to come back, tried to convince her we could make it work. The thing was, as long as I was in the military, she didn't want to be married to me. And once you're in the military, you can't get out until the term you signed up for is over."

"No, you can't. Balancing job and family can be so hard, especially when you're in the military. You're called to serve your country. They won't even let you go home for the birth of your baby, not if you're out to sea. That's what you sign up for. Didn't she know that when she married you?"

"She thought she understood it and could handle it, but she couldn't really. It was all like a culture shock to her. She was a little sheltered to begin with. She had these illusions of what marriage would be like. Reality was much different."

"I'm sorry, Jack. I can tell all this still affects you."

"I guess the good thing that came out of this was that it brought me to my knees and led me back to church. I hit rock bottom after she left me. I didn't know where else to look for help until my friend introduced me to the Navy chaplain. He really helped to point me in the right direction. I started going to church again and slowly got my life back together. The next year, I became a SEAL. I found a lot of purpose in serving my country that way."

"Everyone needs to feel like they've found their purpose. When I used to work in public relations, I thought I was doing what I loved. I was good at it. But when I started this nonprofit, I just knew I was in the place God had called me to be. I was just sorry that I had to lose Andrew to realize my calling."

Jack caught her gaze. She would never understand how her words had impacted him. He felt the same way. Why did his marriage have to end before he realized he'd found his place in life? He knew that God didn't honor divorce, but he'd tried everything he could to win Jennifer back. She was dead set on marrying someone else. Through those trials, he'd found a ministry, though.

"What are you thinking about, Rachel?" he finally asked.

She offered a weak smile. "I was thinking that I'm glad you shared that with me. Thank you."

"Thanks for listening."

"I'm also thinking about the day care you have at Eyes. I like how you've made everything so family oriented. I guess I understand a little bit more about why you've done that now."

"I want to keep families together, not pull them apart."

Her gaze fluttered toward him. She reached over and squeezed his hand. "I think that's great."

As quickly as her hand appeared, she just as quickly pulled it back over into her lap. Jack liked the feeling of her fingers against his. He liked their conversations and being with her. He swallowed, his throat dry. He'd done what he'd vowed not to do. He was starting to fall in love.

"I hope Olivia is doing okay."

Jack slipped a glance at her, turning his thoughts back to their conversation...or at least attempting to. "What do you mean?"

Rachel shrugged. "She didn't seem like herself today. Said she wasn't feeling well. Allergies."

Funny, Jack never remembered Olivia mentioning anything about allergies before. He knew a lot of people were bothered with them at this time of year, though. He began slowing down as they approached the gates at headquarters. "She's had a rough time since her son died. She misses him terribly."

"That's what she was telling me. At least she has her grandchildren. She said they mean the world to her. It's just too bad they don't live closer." She squinted at an oncoming car.

"What's wrong?"

Rachel's head swiveled to follow the car that had just passed them. "That was Olivia who just left."

Jack looked at the clock on his dashboard. 3:21. "It's not time for her to leave yet."

"Jack, I dropped Aidan off with her. If Olivia's not with him, then who..."

Jack swerved around and quickly caught up with her sedan. As he approached the vehicle, Olivia sped up. All of his senses went on red alert, screaming that something was wrong.

"What's going on? Why would she leave?" Rachel shook her head. Her hands went to her stomach as if she might get sick.

Jack pulled his cell phone out and dialed Luke's number. "I need you to look for Aidan. Olivia just left. Do you know anything about this?"

"I'll look into it."

Suddenly, out of the back window of Olivia's car, Aidan's head popped up. Rachel gasped. "She's got Aidan!"

Jack sped up until he was at the car's bumper. Rachel's hands went to the dashboard as if she wanted to reach through the window and grab her son.

"What are you going to do? You're not going to run into them, are you? Don't hurt him!"

Jack had no intention of hurting anyone. He jerked into the next lane and came up beside Olivia's car. He tried to see Olivia's face but couldn't. She stared straight ahead, both hands gripping the wheel. She leaned forward, close to the windshield.

Jack had no choice. He had to stop the car somehow. He accelerated until he was in front of Olivia's car. Then he swerved and slammed on brakes. The SUV skidded to a halt in front of Olivia's car.

Jack heard tires burning against asphalt. Olivia's sedan stopped just inches away from his SUV. But everyone was safe.

Jack and Rachel both jumped from the vehicle at the same time. Rachel ran to the passenger door of Olivia's car.

"Rachel!" Jack warned. Olivia could have a gun for all they knew.

She didn't listen. She jerked the door open and pulled Aidan into her arms. Jack opened the other door and pulled Olivia from the car. He looked her dead in the eye. "Olivia, what are you doing? Have you lost your mind?"

The woman's eyes welled with tears. She shook her head, moaning. "I'm sorry. I'm so sorry."

He loosened his grip. "What's going on, Olivia? You need to start talking, because it looks like you were just kidnapping a child."

"Oh, Jack. I'm so sorry. I didn't know what else to do."

"What do you mean?" Jack asked.

"They said if I didn't bring Aidan to them, then they'd kill my grandchildren!"

Rachel still hugged Aidan to her as she sat in Jack's office, listening again to Olivia share her story.

"I stopped at a red light and this man jumped in the backseat. He put a gun to my head and said that if I didn't leave with Aidan today that he was going to kill my grandchildren. I didn't know what to do!"

"So you were going to let them kill Aidan?" Rachel asked, putting her hands over Aidan's ears so he wouldn't hear their conversation. "How could you do something like that?"

Get 2 Books FREE!

Love Inspired® Books,
a leading publisher of inspirational romance fiction, presents

RIVETING INSPIRATIONAL ROMANCE

A series of edge-of-your-seat suspense novels that reinforce important lessons about life, faith and love!

FREE BOOKS!
Get two free books by acclaimed, inspirational authors!

FREE GIFTS!
Get two exciting surprise gifts absolutely free!

2 FREE BOOKS

RIVETING INSPIRATIONAL ROMANCE

▲ To get your 2 free books and 2 free gifts, affix this peel-off sticker to the reply card and mail it today!

LISUS-LA-11B

Love Inspired.
SUSPENSE
RIVETING INSPIRATIONAL ROMANCE

YES! Please send me the 2 FREE Love Inspired® Suspense books and 2 free gifts for which I qualify. I understand that I am under no obligation to purchase anything further, as explained on the back of this card.

affix
free
books
sticker
here

❏ I prefer the regular-print edition
123/323 IDL FENA

❏ I prefer the larger-print edition
110/310 IDL FENA

Please Print

FIRST NAME

LAST NAME

ADDRESS

APT.#   CITY

STATE/PROV.   ZIP/POSTAL CODE

▼ **DETACH AND MAIL CARD TODAY!** ▼

® and ™ are trademarks owned and used by the trademark owner and/or its licensee.
© 2011 LOVE INSPIRED BOOKS
Printed in the U.S.A.

LISUS-LA-11B

The Reader Service – Here's How it Works:

Jack's gaze flickered to Rachel, his expression a mixture of compassion and concern. His gaze lingered on her a moment before he turned back to Olivia. "What was their next instruction to you, Olivia? Where were you supposed to take him?"

"They didn't say! They said I'd receive further instruction later." She buried her face in her hands. "I just didn't know what to do. I waited until the other children were picked up so I could know they were taken care of. Then I left with Aidan. Told him we were going for ice cream. Please forgive me."

Jack turned to Denton. "We need to get some men over to Tennessee to watch over Olivia's grandchildren, to make sure nothing happens to them."

"How did they know who I was? It was like they'd been watching me. They knew my car. They knew my route to work, when I left, that I had grandchildren."

Rachel's heart panged with unwanted compassion. She didn't want to feel sorry for the woman who'd just tried to kidnap her son, but at the same time she could relate to Olivia's words. She felt the same way.

"Jack, we have a problem." Luke stopped in the doorway.

"What is it?"

"One of the SUVs leaving headquarters was just bombed."

FIFTEEN

Aidan leaned from his booster seat into Rachel's arms, easily going to sleep as they rolled down the road. The sky was midnight black and the air still as stifling in the middle of the night as it was during the day.

There was no conversation during the drive. Just silence. What else could you say when it felt like all means of protection had been exhausted? Even Jack seemed quieter than usual. Rachel saw his jaw flexing, saw his tight grip on the steering wheel.

Luke and Denton followed behind them. In the cover of night, it would be easy to spot any approaching headlights, to know if they were being followed. At least, that's what Rachel told herself.

She had no idea where they were going. She didn't care. All she could think about was staying safe. As it happened every time they ventured away from the headquarters, her stomach was in knots, her hands trembled and sweat covered her brow.

Where was her faith? she wondered. Shouldn't she be trusting God? That He would take care of them? Didn't the Bible warn against worry? But how could she not worry when her life and the life of her son were in danger?

Eventually, exhaustion must have gotten the best of her,

because she drifted to sleep. Not a restful sleep, but sleep kept coming in snatches. Roads surrounded by woods became highways surrounded by strip malls, streets surrounded by houses, and eventually they rumbled down gravel lanes as the landscape became hilly.

She felt the humming of the motor die and pulled her eyes open. Through a sleep-dazed state, she saw a rambling house before them. Uncle Arnold's, she realized. One of several homes he owned, but she did remember coming here a couple of times. He usually resided in his apartment up near the Pentagon in D.C.

Jack glanced in the backseat. "You awake?"

Rachel nodded and yawned. She was more exhausted than she originally thought. Every one of her muscles seemed to ache at the moment. She rolled her head back, trying to get the kinks out of her neck.

Jack nodded toward the house. "Luke and Denton are clearing us before we go inside. It will just be a few more minutes."

"Uncle Arnold's, huh?"

"He volunteered the space. It's ideal, I must say. There's no one around for miles, and a fence surrounds the entire property. There's a state-of-the-art alarm system. No one knows we're here except Luke and Denton. And your uncle, of course."

She nodded, too exhausted to think of any other response. She just wanted to feel safe, to know that Aidan's life wasn't in danger. Was that possible?

A few minutes later, Luke strutted out from the front door. He approached the SUV and nodded. The property was cleared. And so a new chapter began, Rachel thought wearily.

She climbed out, walked around the car to the opposite door and lifted Aidan from his booster seat. He slumbered peacefully in her arms as Jack guided her inside. Jack showed her to a room that looked like it could have been decorated especially for Aidan. She laid him in bed, pulled up the covers and kissed his forehead. Jack waited in the doorway.

"If anything touches the window, an alarm will go off. Luke and Denton will monitor the perimeter in shifts. There are also cameras set up all around the grounds, so we'll be keeping our eyes on things from the inside."

Rachel nodded. Jack really had thought of everything, and Rachel had no doubt that he took this assignment very seriously. She appreciated his dedication and concern.

With his hand on her back, Jack led her down the hallway. "This is where you can stay. I'll bring up your bags and leave them outside the door for you."

Rachel glanced up at him, at his towering, brooding frame that seemingly could protect giants. She grabbed his hand and squeezed it. "Thank you, Jack. For everything." Her throat went dry as she realized how much she enjoyed feeling his fingers beneath hers. He was becoming more than a bodyguard to her, she realized, whether she liked it or not.

"I'm just doing my job."

Rachel released his hand, snapping back to reality. Reality, at the moment, felt like a bucket of cold water to the heart.

Of course Jack was just doing his job. What did she think? That he was falling in love with her? The thought was ridiculous, caused obviously by her heightened emotions. Deep inside, perhaps she did long for a protector and a provider for the family. She'd been silly to think Jack would be that man.

"Of course." She cleared her throat and looked away. "I need to get some sleep. Goodnight, Jack."

She slipped into her room before Jack could see any of the emotions she was sure flashed across her face. She couldn't let him know how much his words had hurt.

* * *

Why had he said that?

Jack gritted his teeth as he walked back down to the SUV to get Rachel's luggage.

Rachel had just been standing there, looking so lovely and vulnerable in the shadows of the hallway. When her fingers intertwined with his, it had brought up too many old emotions. He remembered how he'd failed Jennifer. He didn't want to ever do that to another woman he cared about.

And he had to be honest with himself—he was starting to care about Rachel in terms that were more than merely professional.

He stepped out into the night, and the sound of crickets singing their song immediately enveloped him. Vice Admiral Harris's home was beautiful and just what they needed—secluded, unexpected and a safe respite, at least for a few days.

He grabbed the few bags that Rachel had packed. She had so few possessions with her. He'd tried to provide what he could, but he knew that nothing compared to having your own clothes and belongings, especially when you were desperate for comfort.

But there had been no opportunity to grab those items. Between Rachel's house being ransacked and the threats to Olivia and Aidan, Jack knew he had to leave and fast. The terrorists knew where Rachel was and they were desperate to play games with her.

The question was, why did they want to scare her so badly? It almost seemed like their goal was simply to scare her. But that didn't fit Apaka's modus operandi. Everyone else on the list had simply been killed, not threatened beforehand.

Perhaps this woman who had sent Andrew letters would have some of the answers they needed.

As Jack stepped back toward the house, he glanced up

and spotted Rachel standing on the second-story balcony. She didn't appear to see him. Instead, her gaze fixated on something in the distance. The rolling hills, perhaps? Jack knew the past twenty-four hours had put a strain on her. He could even see it now in the solemn expression she wore.

He looked away and gave her some privacy. Inside, he climbed the stairs and set her bags outside her door. He then peeked in on Aidan, just to make sure the boy was okay. He'd been such a trouper throughout everything. He had to admit that being with Rachel and Aidan had stirred up some kind of longing within him. He liked feeling like they all belonged together—like a family.

When he was sure Aidan was okay, he turned to find Luke and Denton. As he passed the door to the balcony, he paused. Should he even interrupt Rachel? Perhaps she wanted to be alone. Or perhaps she needed someone to talk to...

He stood at the door, contemplating what to do.

Earlier he'd said he was just doing his job. His job wasn't to protect her emotions. Yet that's exactly what he desired to do. To protect her inside and out, physically, and emotionally and spiritually.

Why was doing this job so hard sometimes?

He remained at the doorway another moment, his desires toying with him while his responsibilities smacked him in the face. Was there even a win-win in this situation?

A pleasant breeze fanned Rachel's face. She knew they were in the foothills of the Blueridge Mountains, and she welcomed the change in temperature. The fresh, crisp air helped to clear her head a little.

After she'd said good-night to Jack, she stood in her temporary bedroom for a moment, simply staring at it. The thought of lying down and trying to find the sleep that had once felt so demanding seemed impossible. She needed a breath of fresh air, a moment to try to process everything.

She leaned against the railing and replayed the image of Aidan's face staring at her from the back window of Olivia's car. What if it hadn't been Olivia who'd taken him? What if it had been a terrorist? What if they hadn't gotten him back?

A tear rolled down her cheek. She quickly wiped it with the back of her hand.

Why was she crying? None of that had happened. Her heart should be overflowing with joy that they'd been victorious. She needed to get a grip, to stay strong. Yet the tears kept coming. And the images of Aidan kept replaying over and over. The what-ifs repeated themselves.

A footfall sounded behind her. Ever so quiet. Almost imagined.

But it wasn't.

She sucked in a breath. Apaka. What if it was an Apaka operative? She needed a weapon. Something. Her gaze scanned her immediate surroundings.

Nothing.

"Rachel."

She twirled around. Jack. It was Jack's voice. Relief rushed through her. Jack stepped from the shadows, his gaze accessing her, as he often did.

Rachel quickly wiped at her face again, trying to get rid of the evidence that she'd been crying. It didn't work.

"I just thought I'd check on you," he said quietly. He stepped beside her.

Rachel turned back toward the breeze and nodded. Her chin trembled, though, belying her true feelings. No more saying, "I'm fine." She looked into the distant darkness. "I've been trying really hard not to feel sorry for myself throughout this whole process. It's not working right now."

"You're not feeling sorry for yourself, Rachel. You've just

been through a lot. You've been processing everything very well."

"It's just that…when I saw Aidan…" Her voice caught.

Jack slipped his arms around her. She let herself cry there. She didn't care anymore. She was tired of trying to be strong, of trying to constantly be in control of her life, her emotions. She just had to let go and trust God.

"I'm sorry, Rachel. I wish you didn't have to go through this."

It felt good to have Jack's strong arms around her, holding her up, to hear his words of comfort. But she knew having his arms around her was making her dream about a life she couldn't have. He'd made that clear only moments earlier. Was he trying to toy with her emotions? Is that why he'd taken another step forward after he'd just taken a step back?

No, she remembered, he wasn't toying with her. He was doing his job.

She stepped back and felt Jack's intense gaze on her.

Before he could say anything else or remind her of the nature of their relationship, she hurried inside, desperate to protect her heart.

SIXTEEN

Jack awoke early the next morning and went to the kitchen to cook breakfast. He'd tossed and turned most of the night. Though he knew Luke and Denton were keeping their eyes on the place, there was something unsettling about being here.

Maybe it was simply his close proximity to Rachel?

He'd wanted to go after her last night when she'd fled from the balcony. He'd wanted to explain his words, his actions. But instead he'd remained tethered where he was by some unseen weight from his past.

He'd only intended to go to the balcony and check on Rachel. But then he'd seen the tears rolling down her cheeks. The sight had done something strange to his heart. Pulling her into his arms had only seemed natural.

Answers were eluding them, and it was obviously starting to get to Rachel. He couldn't blame her. He'd seen her heart break when she spotted Aidan in Olivia's car. How could it not? Apaka was getting to people, turning innocents into their workhorses. Jack didn't like it one bit.

Luke trotted downstairs, already looking fresh and energized. He grabbed a mug from the cabinet. "Just want to grab some coffee."

"How's the surveillance going?"

"Haven't seen another car pass by since we got here."

Jack nodded and poured some coffee into Luke's mug. "Good. That's what I want to hear."

Luke surveyed the kitchen. "You making breakfast for us?"

Jack raised an eyebrow and flipped another pancake. He couldn't remember the last time he'd actually cooked breakfast instead of simply eating cereal. "I'm trying to keep everyone occupied and their thoughts off of the events at hand."

"Denton's about to take over a new shift so I can get some shuteye. I have to say that I feel good about being here. Maybe we're finally a step ahead of Apaka."

"I'm not so sure."

Luke paused, his coffee mug halfway to his lips. "Why would you say that?"

"They've always been a step ahead of us. The only way that's possible is if there's an inside man. I need you to look into that for me. Find out if there's anyone suspicious at Eyes. I know we do extensive background checks on anyone before we hire them, but I need to know if anyone is hiding something."

"Yes, sir."

"I need it done ASAP."

"I'm on it." Luke grabbed his coffee and stepped back toward the dining room where all of their computers had been set up.

As Jack continued to flip pancakes and keep an eye on the bacon, his thoughts wandered to Rachel and Aidan again. Aidan was just like Andrew in so many ways. Jack's thoughts went back to Afghanistan when he first befriended Andrew. In the beginning, he'd only struck up a friendship because of his assignment. Eventually, it had grown into the real deal, though.

He remembered being in the barracks when Andrew pulled out some letters from his pocket and began reading them aloud. Rachel's words had been eloquent. They'd given Andrew hope in his final days.

Jack had known when he listened to Andrew read those letters that Rachel was special. Someone who could express herself so beautifully and bring so much hope to others had to be special. He considered Andrew one lucky guy.

But Andrew had something dark about him, also, something he was hiding. Had Rachel suspected that? Did she know anything was wrong? And could Jack be the one to break it to her?

They'd had very few conversations about Andrew. Jack feared that she might ask too many questions, questions he didn't want to answer. But the time was drawing near when he was going to have to. He'd have to own up to his role in her husband's death. Once he shared those things, Rachel would never welcome his embrace again. Even acting like they were a couple to protect her would be out of the question.

His heart fell at the thought.

Why did it have to be Rachel? Why did she have to be Andrew's wife? Why did her life have to be in danger right now?

He sighed. He could put some distance between himself and Rachel while at headquarters. In this house, and with so few men here, it would be impossible.

Just as Jack flipped the last pancake, he looked up and spotted Rachel and Aidan in the doorway. "Morning," he muttered.

Aidan sucked in a gasp of air. "Are you making pancakes, Mr. Jack?"

Jack couldn't help but grin. "I sure am. Do you like pancakes?"

"Almost as much as I like macaroni and cheese!"

Aidan scrambled from his mother's arms and promptly sat at the table and grabbed his fork. Jack dared to glance up at Rachel as he approached with their breakfast. He wasn't sure what she was thinking about him. From the way she was avoiding his gaze, she wasn't feeling too friendly.

That was okay. He just had to keep her safe. That's what he told himself, at least.

They kept the conversation superficial while they ate— mostly centered on Aidan. When they finished, Rachel sent Aidan to watch some cartoons so she could cleanup the kitchen. Jack stayed around to help. Silence fell between them as Rachel washed and he dried. He glanced around the enormous kitchen for a minute, trying to think of something to talk about that didn't involve terrorists, Andrew or the hit list.

"So, your uncle really makes this much money working for the Department of Defense?"

Rachel shrugged and handed him a plate. "My impression has always been that Uncle Arnold comes from old money. Although, I do think he makes a decent living doing his job. He's always been one of my biggest supporters over at Operation 26 Letters."

"How did he become friends with your family?"

"He and my father went to college together at Yale. They remained close ever after."

"I see."

She stopped and looked at him. "You don't have to pretend, Jack."

"What do you mean?"

"You don't have to make small talk or pretend to be interested in my life. It's okay."

"Who said I was pretending?"

Rachel shook her head. "Jack, I've appreciated your support. Not only have you been my guardian, but by default you've also been a confidante. I apologize for that. I shouldn't have ever put you in that position. So from here on out, don't feel obligated."

"But Rachel—"

"Really, it's okay, Jack. Just do your job. That's all anyone expects from you."

And before he could say anything else, she walked away.

Rachel and Aidan spent the rest of the day playing games, watching videos and trying to keep themselves occupied in whatever way possible. Jack hovered nearby, keeping one eye on the TV monitors that showed the perimeter of the house. Rachel decided she was glad she'd taken a moment to speak point-blank to Jack. She had to protect her emotions, and it was too hard to do that with Jack so close. So she'd keep her distance.

Halfway through a puzzle, Rachel heard Jack's cell phone ring. She watched curiously as he pulled the phone from his belt and stepped into the kitchen. As always, she tried to interpret his grunts and other noncommittal expressions, but failed. He snapped the phone shut as he stepped back into the room. He went back to viewing the video feed without making eye contact.

Her shoulders sagged. "What is it? Did something else happen?"

Jack glanced over at her. "It was just an update on Meredith."

Rachel straightened, suddenly anxious to answers. "What about her?"

"She is the one the money was being sent to."

Rachel's heart fell. Why would Andrew send her money? Did they have a child together? Were they married at one time? It just didn't make sense...

"We're trying to arrange a meeting."

Rachel leaned toward Jack. "I want to be there."

"We really need to keep your location quiet. The more you leave this house, the higher the chance that Apaka will discover where you are."

"I want to meet her, Jack. I want to look in her eyes."

"You could be looking in the eyes of a terrorist."

"Or I could be looking in the eyes of someone who my husband cheated on me with."

"It won't do you any good to be there for either. What would it solve?"

"You can see the truth in a person's eyes."

"I'm sorry, Rachel. I'm going alone. I'm not going to walk you into what could potentially be a trap."

Rachel's heart sank. Not only was a terrorist organization trying to kill her, but answers that she'd longed to obtain for years were within her reach, yet Jack blocked her from getting them.

"Would you mind sitting with Aidan for a moment?" she asked. "I just need some time by myself to collect my thoughts right now."

"Of course." He nodded. His steady gaze on her made her cheeks burn, however. She really wished he didn't have that affect on her. "Stay inside, please. And away from any windows. Just to be safe, of course."

She nodded and fled upstairs to her room. She walked to her bed, rationalizing that her lack of sleep the night before was doing funny things to her emotions. She stopped at the edge of her bed and stared at it a moment. There was a wrinkle in the covers, as if someone had sat down there.

Had she sat down there to put her shoes on that morning? She shook her head. No, she'd sat in the chair over in the corner. She'd always been picky about keeping a clean house, and especially about making a bed with crisp, taut sheets. She clearly remembered pulling the wrinkles out this morning, using her hand to whisk away any bumps.

Had someone been sitting on her bed? But who? And why?

The next day, Jack left early in the morning to drive up to Washington, D.C., and visit Meredith. His thoughts turned over in his head as he replayed his conversation with Rachel. She'd made it clear that she wanted to keep her distance.

Of course, she probably thought that Jack had made it clear that he wanted to keep his distance.

He'd never intended to hurt her. Perhaps they had gotten too close. What guy in his right mind wouldn't dream, at least for a minute, about dating a woman like Rachel Reynolds? She was beautiful, kind, smart. She loved God. So maybe he'd gotten carried away. But Rachel was right. They should just keep things professional.

Why did that thought cause his heart to thud with sadness then?

He sighed and brushed off the thoughts as he approached the metro area. His GPS informed him that he was getting closer to Meredith's house. He'd kept an eye on the road behind him for the entire trip here and hadn't seen anything suspicious.

Denton stayed back at the house with Rachel and Aidan, and Jack felt certain they were safe with him for the time being. Meanwhile, Luke was back at headquarters, now trying to figure out who the mole was. Jack felt sure there was a mole; he rationalized this to himself as he exited off Interstate 95. Whoever it was had done a great job concealing their divided loyalties. Jack hadn't suspected a thing until the past week or so, and Jack usually considered himself an excellent judge of character.

A few turns later, Jack pulled into a blue-collar neighborhood.

He checked the address again. This was where Meredith O'Connor lived.

As he stepped from the SUV, he glanced around, looking for signs of anything suspicious. Unfortunately, in this area of town, almost everyone looked suspicious. He got a few strange looks of his own.

He could feel his holster around his shoulders and the gun waiting there. He hoped he didn't have to use it. He hoped that Meredith O'Connor didn't have any association with Apaka.

Jack walked up to a wood-sided house and knocked at the door. A moment later, the door cracked open and a woman in her mid-twenties opened the door. She was tall and thin with long, dark hair that stretched nearly to her waist. She didn't smile when she spotted him, and her eyes contained somewhat of a cool assessment.

"Jack Sergeant."

He nodded crisply. "Meredith. Thanks for agreeing to meet with me."

She opened the door wider. Her eyes skittered from side to side as he stepped inside, as if she were waiting for something—or someone—to appear. Jack's guard went up.

The door creaked shut and Jack did a quick assessment of her home. Neat, orderly, slightly folksy. Nothing that would set off any alarms in his head.

Meredith led him to an old couch in the living room. He sat on the edge and waited as she pulled a dining room table chair across from him. She didn't even attempt to smile or offer any warmth.

She drew in a deep breath. "You wanted to meet with me about Andrew."

"We're doing an investigation and exploring his possible connection to a case we're involved with. We came across some letters from you to Andrew, and we're wondering about your relationship with him."

She sighed and looked at her neat, unpolished fingernails. "I was afraid this day might come. I prayed that it wouldn't, however."

"What was your relationship with Andrew Reynolds?"

She looked up and for the first time, Jack saw some sadness in her eyes. "My family all worked with an aid organization over in Afghanistan. That's how we met Andrew. He stopped by sometimes and always tried to keep an eye on us, to make sure we were safe."

"I know that Andrew sent you money before he died, Meredith. I'm trying to figure out why."

Meredith looked down at the fingers twisting in her lap. "He did send us money. But it's not what you think."

"Why don't you explain then?"

"Things were very tight."

"So he was sending money to help support the organization?"

She glanced up and Jack saw the hesitation on her features. "Yes. But there's more to the story than that."

"Go on."

She looked up at him, and Jack could see the strain in her eyes. "You have to understand something, Mr. Sergeant. Andrew sent us money to help support us only because he killed my father."

SEVENTEEN

Rachel had been pacing for the entire morning. She tried to keep herself occupied by playing with Aidan and even doing some cooking, but her mind couldn't stop imagining what kind of conversations Jack might be having right now.

She glanced back at Aidan, who sat at the kitchen table coloring in some new books that Denton had given him this morning. Denton sat in Jack's normal place, watching all of the security video feeds in the dining room. He was pleasant enough—a little warmer and more laid-back than Jack—but he wasn't Jack.

She missed the lighthearted companionship she and Jack had shared. It disappeared since that awkward night—had it only been two nights ago?—when Jack had comforted her and some unseen line had been crossed. That night when he'd admitted that she was just a job to him and she felt foolish for ever dreaming it could be anything more. She felt guilty for even thinking of herself when her son's life could be in danger. It was better that she stay focused. If she needed to express some of her fears, next time she'd simply write in a journal instead of talking to Jack.

"You doing okay, Ms. Reynolds?" Denton stretched in the doorway, a customary toothpick in his mouth. "You seem a little nervous."

"Just anxious to learn what Jack finds out today."

"He should be back any time now."

Rachel leaned against the doorway. "How long have you worked for Jack?"

"Three years. We were SEALs together, so we've known each other for longer."

"Is it hard for him to go from being your equal to being your boss?"

"I couldn't ask for a better leader. He's one in a million. Would give his life for a brother."

Rachel felt her cheeks warm but didn't understand why. She'd sensed after only knowing Jack a day that he was loyal and kind. She'd always felt safe with him. Denton's pronouncement shouldn't have any affect on her, she chided.

"What about Luke? When did he come on?" She simply needed to keep talking, to keep her mind occupied.

"About the same time I did."

"Where has Luke been? I haven't seen him around today."

Denton glanced back at her. "Jack sent him back to Eyes."

"Why?"

"I'm not sure of the details, Ms. Reynolds."

Rachel nodded but knew there was more to the story. If Jack sent someone back to Eyes and back to the possibility of being tracked down on their way to or from their safe house, there had to be a good reason for it. What was Luke doing back at headquarters?

She heard a vehicle rumbling down the gravel driveway. She ran to the window and saw Jack's SUV coming up the lane. She forced herself to stay in the living room and to not run out and greet him as every instinct seemed to scream.

Finally, Jack stepped through the door from the garage. Rachel waited in the living room, her stomach doing flip-flops. As much as she tried to prepare herself for whatever news he might have, she wasn't sure that was even possible.

She tried to read Jack's expression as he stood in the

doorway but couldn't. He nodded toward the kitchen table. Aidan still colored and occupied himself, so Rachel slipped away.

It felt like a weight pressed down on her chest as she sat across from Jack. Would her fears be confirmed? Or was there a plausible explanation for the letters and secret debt? She closed her eyes and lifted up a quick prayer for strength before starting the conversation.

"How did it go?" she dared to ask.

Jack offered a slow, almost uncertain nod. "I think I finally have some answers for you."

It took a moment for her to find her words as her heart raced with a mixture of anxiety and hope. "Then please, share."

"Meredith did know your husband. They met through an aid organization over in Afghanistan. Her entire family was working over there together. They had been working there since Meredith was young. Andrew befriended them through his work as a SEAL. He always tried to pay special attention to the building where their agency was housed. There had been a lot of bombings in that area, and Andrew tried to keep them all safe."

A sick feeling churned in her gut. Was this going where she feared it might? What started as simply protecting her family had turned into a romance? Why waste any more time wondering? She was beyond niceties at this point. "Just tell me, Jack. They had an affair, didn't they?"

He looked at his hands for a moment. "No, actually they didn't, Rachel."

What? If not an affair, then what could their relationship have been? "I don't understand then…"

"Andrew went into Kabul once during some of his free time. Enemy fire broke out. Andrew began firing back. There were some civilians nearby that he was trying to keep safe."

Jack paused. "Meredith's dad accidentally stepped into the line of fire. He died instantly."

Rachel's heart felt like it had stopped. "Andrew killed someone?"

"Mommy?" Aidan pattered into the room with one of his coloring books.

"One minute, sweetie." She raised a finger, instructing him to wait.

Jack's face remained tight. "It was an accident. But he felt terribly about it. Meredith's family decided to report the death being from enemy fire so that Andrew wouldn't face any disciplinary action. It could have meant leave from the military or possibly a trial."

Rachel nodded, still trying to comprehend everything, yet also realizing that there was more to be told. "I see."

"Mommy—" Aidan pulled at her shirt.

"Aidan, one minute. Mommy's talking right now. Please don't interrupt. It's bad manners."

Jack continued. "They knew that Andrew was one of the good guys and they didn't want to penalize him for it. They said he was constantly bringing by toys for the children or helping with donations when they were low on funding. They really thought highly of him, even after the accident."

Rachel heart swelled. That sounded like Andrew. Big hearted. Looking out for others. He must have been devastated by Meredith's father's death. That would explain the apologies and forgiveness and love mentioned in the letters. They'd been Andrew's cry for forgiveness from the family, and Meredith had simply been talking about Andrew's love for their organization.

"What about the money that Andrew sent them?"

"Andrew sent Meredith's family money to try and help them out financially. They were barely making ends meet with their nonprofit, especially after their father was killed. He was trying to help them keep it going."

She swallowed, the saliva burning her throat. That's what those letters had been? That's where the money had gone? Relief washed through her with such force that she wanted to chuckle. "Thank you, Jack. I can't tell you how much relief I feel in finally knowing the truth. Relief and...I don't know. A few other emotions that will take some time to process."

"I'm glad you can finally feel some closure."

Rachel sighed, going back to the bigger problems at hand. Just for a moment she'd forgotten about them, but now they came back to the forefront of her mind, demanding more attention than ever. "I guess there was no connection with the list, however?"

He shook his head. "No, we're no closer to answers than we were before."

And as always, they were at a dead end. The sad part was that the term *dead end* had new meaning to her, with special emphasis on the word *dead*.

"Mommy, I have a question. Please."

She looked down at Aidan. "Yes, what is it?"

"Who did this in my coloring book?"

She looked down at the page. On the inside front cover, someone had drawn a cartoon-like picture of a woman who looked eerily similar to Rachel. Only this woman was crying and had a gun pointed to her head. In a bubble beside her face were written, "It's almost time."

She looked up at Jack and saw the alarm in his gaze.

How had Apaka gotten a hold of Aidan's coloring book? Unless they'd been in the house.

EIGHTEEN

"Jack, we've got a problem."

Denton's voice caused Jack's spine to straighten. He forgot about the picture for a moment and hurried across the room to the computer monitors. "What's going on?"

Denton pointed to one of the screens. "Right there. Behind that tree. There's a man. With a gun."

Jack squinted at the black-and-white image until the man came into focus. He wore camouflage and a face mask, blending right in with the environment. If it hadn't been for the sun's reflection off of the barrel of his gun, Jack would have never noticed him.

Jack looked at the other screens, looking for any other telltale signs of intruders. There, on the opposite side of the house, was another man, also holding a gun. "They've found us," he muttered.

"Apaka? Apaka has found us?" Rachel's eyes widened as big as saucers. She pulled Aidan to her.

"You two, get down behind the couch and stay there until we say move." Jack pulled the gun from its holster. "I'd say we have a serious problem, Denton."

"I'd agree." Denton pulled his gun out just as a shot shattered the front window.

The two men locked gazes, both realizing that a battle for their lives was about to begin. Jack needed a battle plan and quick. "Who knows how many operatives are out there? We've got to get out of here and now, or we're just going to be sitting ducks."

"I'll get the car, but first I need to clear the garage, make sure no one has infiltrated the house yet," Denton muttered.

"Jack, what's going on?" Rachel's voice sounded thin, fragile. Jack glanced back at the security feed.

"There are at least three men out there. Maybe more. At this point, they're not even being shy about being here."

"The garage is clear!" Denton shouted from the other room. "Come on!"

"Stay low," Jack ordered Rachel and Aidan. Another bullet splintered the wall. "But move fast."

Rachel shielded Aidan with her own body as they crawled along the floor. How had they found out their location? No one had followed Jack today. He was sure of it. But somehow, they'd been found. All kinds of theories began brewing in Jack's head. He'd have to sort them out later. Right now, they had to concentrate on getting out of here.

Glass shattered in the other room. That time it sounded like a vase or a picture, perhaps. Jack didn't care—as long as it wasn't Rachel or Aidan. Denton stood at the door, partly crouched, waving them over with a certain urgency.

As soon as Aidan was close enough, Denton grabbed the boy and rushed him to the SUV. Rachel was right behind him, scrambling for the safe confines of the vehicle. As Jack climbed into the SUV, Rachel pulled the seatbelt over Aidan, her hands trembling as she did so.

"Denton, you drive." Jack held up his gun. "I'll hold them off."

"Got it."

Jack looked back at Rachel and Aidan. "Rachel, whatever you do, stay down. And pray. Pray hard."

Rachel trembled still but nodded.

A crash sounded inside. Was that the front door being knocked down? Jack didn't wait around to find out. "Let's go!"

The SUV squealed from its home, busting through the garage door. As soon as sunlight hit the hood, bullets peppered the vehicle. The front windshield shattered at the impact of the bullets. Jack raised his gun.

He looked back at the porch, saw a man crouching there. The man's gun pointed straight at them. Jack shot, aiming at the man's hand. He must have hit. The man's weapon dropped to the ground.

But not before another operative fired. The bullet hit their tire. There was a loud band, then a whoosh of air followed by a *flap, flap, flap.*

Lord, help us.

The vehicle swerved to the left before overcorrecting and teetering to the right. Rachel toppled into the door, still grasping Aidan and covering him. Pieces of glass rained throughout the vehicle.

"Keep going! We've got to keep going!" Jack shouted.

"I'm on it." Denton charged forward, though the vehicle leaned lopsided. Those defensive driving courses at Eyes had paid off.

Jack looked back, at the men surrounding the house—now all staring at and focusing on their fleeing SUV. "You see anybody ahead of us?"

"Negative. This was all obviously planned, though. It wouldn't surprise me if there were more men out there just waiting."

Jack stared at the security gate that they were quickly approaching at the end of the driveway. "We've got to open that gate. The SUV won't be able to break through it like the garage door. It's steel and meant to withstand impact."

"The code is 9-25-38."

"We're going to have to move fast. Who knows if there are more of them out there." Jack glanced into the woods surrounding the property. He prayed this wasn't another trap. Slowing down at all was risky, but they had no other choice.

"Jack?" Rachel asked from the backseat.

He turned his head toward her. "Listen, we've got to open this gate. Stay down. We're not out of danger yet. Understand?"

"Understand."

Jack slowly exhaled, praying God would give him speed, quick fingers and a moment of invisibility.

Rachel looked down at Aidan and saw that his wide eyes were brimming with tears. The other times they'd been in danger, he'd viewed it as an adventure. This time, it was getting to him. Rachel's heart twisted.

Flap, flap, flap. The deflated tire sounded its distress as the car slowed.

"We've got to make this quick," Jack muttered.

Rachel heard the window going down, heard the beep of numbers on the keypad outside of the gate. *Lord, be with us.* How many times had she uttered that prayer today? In the past two weeks? Since Andrew died, for that matter?

"Got it!" Jack exclaimed.

Just as the gates groaned outside the window, another bullet shattered the glass behind them. Rachel screamed as more bits of glass sprinkled them. Denton gunned the engine and charged away from the property.

"You've been hit," Denton said.

"It just grazed my arm," Jack muttered.

Jack had been shot? How bad was his injury? Had it really just grazed his arm? "Jack?" Adrenaline pulsed through Rachel.

"I'm fine, Rachel. We've got bigger worries at the moment."

Another bullet hit the rearview mirror. Rachel hovered over Aidan. She pressed her head into the back of the leather seat as the SUV veered to the left again. How long could they drive on the tire rim? Were there more men out in these woods just waiting for them to stop so they could attack? And if there were, would they survive? Her heart twisted again. She had to think positive.

"We've got to make it into the town at least," Jack said.

"How far away is town?"

"Ten miles."

Ten miles? On a blown out tire? Rachel kissed the top of Aidan's head. She looked up again just in time to see a man in camouflage step in the middle of the street, his gun aimed straight at them.

NINETEEN

"Get down!" Jack shouted.

He raised his gun, aimed it out the broken windshield and shot the man's shoulder. The operative fell to the ground, grasping his injury. His body stretched across the narrow road. Denton swerved to miss him. Before he could right the vehicle, they scraped a tree and careened into a ditch.

Jack hit the dashboard on impact. He sat up and looked into the backseat. "Everyone okay?"

Rachel raised her head. "I think so. Aidan, are you okay?"

The little boy nodded, looking slightly dazed.

Denton had a fresh knot on his forehead. Jack didn't have time to contemplate everyone's injuries—minor as they were—at the moment. His gaze raced to the operative he'd just shot. The man lay in the middle of the road, still writhing. But the man's eyes were fixed on the gun that had skittered across the road.

"Denton, scan the rest of the area for more operatives. I've got him." Jack avoided his crushed door and climbed through the broken window. As soon as his feet hit the ground, he darted toward the man.

The operative gained his strength surprisingly fast and leapt to his feet. He lunged for the gun, but Jack reached it first. He kicked it out of reach before pulling out his own gun and aiming it at the man.

"Where are your cohorts?" Jack demanded.

The man's face twisted in a mixture of pain and disgust. "Wouldn't you like to know."

"I'd suggest you start talking."

The man eyed Jack's gun. "Never!"

He lunged forward with surprising strength and snatched the gun from Jack's hand. Before Jack could react, the man turned the gun toward himself and pulled the trigger. Jack looked away from his dead body, hoping that Aidan hadn't just witnessed that. He glanced toward the SUV and saw Rachel shielding the boy's face. Her own eyes were wide with disbelief. He wished he had time to comfort her, but he didn't.

He hurried toward the SUV. "Come on, we've got to get out of here. Is everyone okay?"

Rachel's gaze zoomed in on his wound. "You're bleeding, Jack."

"Don't worry about me."

"You need to get someone to look at that."

He shrugged it off, ignoring the pain hammering through his arm. "No time for that now. We need to go." His gaze scanned the woods. "There could be more men out there. Every second counts."

"Where are we going?" Rachel asked.

"Through the woods. If we stay on the road, we're easy targets. The woods will give us some cover, at least." He glanced down at Rachel's flip-flops. They'd only had time to flee in what they were wearing. Those shoes would be a hindrance walking through the thick underbrush, however. He glanced at Aidan, realizing there was no way Rachel would be able to carry him. "Aidan, want to ride on my back?"

The boy raised his head and nodded with a bit of uncertainty.

"You've got to hold on tight, though, okay?"

He nodded again.

"Jack—" Rachel started.

"Rachel, we've got to move fast. Do you understand?"

She opened her mouth to speak but closed it again. Her eyes were wells of emotion, though. "Okay." She helped Aidan climb onto Jack's back.

Then they stepped into the thick woods, that instantly swallowed them with its thick foliage. Good for them to hide, but also good for any Apaka operatives to take cover and ambush them. Jack had a bad feeling about this. He instructed Rachel to stay behind him and Denton to bring up the tail.

Jack pointed in the distance. "We'll head west. We'll cut some time off the trek to town this way."

Rachel moved a branch out of the way and stayed close behind him. "What then? What happens when we get into town?"

"Then we get a new car and take off to where no one can find us."

"And we stay there until they find us?"

Jack glanced back at her, wishing he could assure her that her thoughts were unfounded, born out of paranoia and fear. But were they? He couldn't guarantee it.

"We need to keep moving." He motioned forward.

Rachel picked up on the fact that Jack didn't answer her question. She said nothing. She knew the risky situation they were in and didn't need it spelled out. They weren't going to be safe anywhere until this cell of Apaka was all captured or dead.

Her foot twisted on the rocky terrain of the woods as they hurried over a dry creek bed. She found her footing and rushed ahead. If only she'd been wearing sneakers and jeans today. But instead she'd dressed for the warm weather in jean shorts, a T-shirt and flip-flops.

Branches scratched at her legs, and her shoes couldn't get a good grip on the slick forest floor. But it didn't matter right now. What mattered was that Aidan was safe, that Apaka didn't find them.

She knew Jack's arm was injured, yet he toted Aidan on his back. Aidan clung to him, and Rachel knew her son felt safe with Jack, much like she'd felt safe with her dad as a child. Her heart panged with sadness for a moment. Was Jack becoming a father figure to Aidan? How would he feel once Jack was gone from their lives? How would Rachel feel?

She had to admit one thing—Jack was a true soldier, not letting the pain slow him down. But Rachel worried about both Jack and Aidan. Jack needed medical help. Aidan...well, Rachel simply wished she could magically transport him out of this situation.

"What does it look like back there, Denton?" Jack asked.

"I don't see anything. But I don't like this. I have a feeling all of those operatives who were at the house are now trying to track us through these woods."

Fear sizzled up Rachel's spine, and her chest tightened. How would they get out of this one, if not only by God's grace?

"You okay, Rachel?" Jack asked. "You hanging in?"

She nodded, even though she realized he wasn't looking at her. She couldn't seem to make the words leave her mouth, though.

"Rachel?"

She sucked in a shallow breath, steadying herself by holding on to a boulder for a moment. "I'm...I'm fine."

"You're doing great. Stay as close to me as you can, okay?"

She nodded again. Jack had Aidan, so there was no keeping her away. She'd sprain her ankle if she had to, if it meant staying close to her son. Denton stayed close behind her, obviously guarding her from any unseen dangers.

Suddenly, she didn't feel him behind her anymore. She paused. "Denton?"

She turned in time to see him raise his gun and fire. A grunt sounded in the distance, and Rachel saw a tangle of leaves and branches moving. A man—an operative—must have collapsed there. She froze a moment.

"We've got to keep going," Denton said, urging her along.

She ran a hand through her hair, felt the glass crystals from the shattered windshield tumbling out. All it would take was one moment for her world to tumble. One moment for a bullet to come from nowhere and destroy life. One moment for her to meet her Creator.

Don't think like that, Rachel. You're going to get out of this.

She shoved another branch aside. Her legs were scratched and bleeding. Her feet ached, and at least one toe had been skinned raw on a jagged rock. But Aidan was safe. That was all that mattered. Maybe the rest of the operatives wouldn't find them.

"I see three men ahead, Denton," Jack muttered. "We've got to take cover."

"There's a rock wall over there. Maybe a cave in it? Somewhere that would provide shelter for a few minutes."

"Let's head that way."

The tightness in Rachel's chest only intensified, and her heart beat erratically. A cave? Where was a cave? Her gaze searched her surroundings, looking for a place of solitude and safety. All she saw were trees and boulders and leaves.

Suddenly, Denton threw his body over hers. She heard wood splinter, heard another bullet fly, heard another groan. Aidan? Jack?

She looked up and saw that Jack had his gun in hand. He'd taken down another operative. They were okay. They were both okay. Her heart rate slowed for a moment.

Three down now. How many more to go?

Jack pulled her to her feet using only one of his strong arms. The other held Aidan, despite his injury. "You okay?"

Her ribs ached, her head pounded, her throat was dry, but she was fine. "Thank you." She looked at Denton, who brushed the dirt from his slacks. "Thank you both."

"Mommy?" Aidan looked at her with those wide, innocent eyes.

"Mommy's right here, baby. I'm fine. You doing okay?"

His chin trembled. "I'm scared."

"I know, honey. It's okay to be scared sometimes. Just hold on to Mr. Jack, okay? Use your superpowers and pretend to be invisible. That way the bad guys won't see you."

That seemed to satisfy him. His lips drew in a tight line and he closed his eyes, as if willing himself to be unseen. Maybe that would help him get through the next few minutes at least.

"The wall's right up ahead. We'll take cover there and take out the rest of the men before we finish the rest of the journey. You think you can make it?" Jack looked down at her legs, that she knew looked like she'd been through a battlefield at this point.

She nodded. "I'll do whatever it takes."

They found the rock wall a few minutes later. And there, right at the base of it, was a boulder. They could all fit behind it and it would offer them some shelter, for a few minutes at least.

Jack made sure that Rachel and Aidan were pressed into the rocks, securely behind the massive boulder, before he met with Denton a few feet away. His gaze scanned the surroundings as they spoke, looking for any approaching danger.

"I think you should stay here with them, make sure they're protected," Denton said. "I'll survey the area, try to spot the operatives before they spot us. It's our only chance of getting out of this intact. We can't outrun them at this point."

"I was thinking the same thing," Jack said. He didn't want to let Rachel and Aidan out of his sight, so staying with them was his first choice also. "My guess is that there are three more men, maybe four. I'll keep an eye on Rachel and Aidan, and let them rest a bit. They need to get some of their energy back."

"Sounds like a plan."

"Be careful, Denton."

Denton looked around the woods and veered to the right, crouching low as he moved swiftly. His training as a SEAL would come in handy right now and would be much easier to execute alone than with Rachel and Aidan.

Jack went back to the boulder and checked on Rachel and Aidan. Rachel leaned against the rock wall, her head resting on it, while Aidan sat cuddled in her lap. Jack quickly assessed Rachel's injuries. All the cuts and scrapes on her legs looked minor, but she'd still need some first aid on them. Aidan appeared uninjured physically. Jack was sure the incident had shaken him up, though.

He needed to keep both of their thoughts occupied, to at least give them a moment of relief. He crouched in front of them and rested his elbows on his legs. "Has anyone seen Aidan?"

Rachel smiled wearily and raised her head. "He's invisible, remember? We'll never find him."

"That's right. I wonder where he is? He could be anywhere right now and we wouldn't even know it."

"It's true. That's one of the advantages to being invisible, I guess. Must be nice."

"I'm right here!" Aidan triumphantly popped out of his mom's arms.

"Did you hear that?" Rachel asked. "It sounded like Aidan."

"I'm right here, Mommy! Right here!"

She looked at him and grinned. "I knew you'd be close by!"

Jack smiled and ruffled the boy's hair. He lowered himself to a seated position at the entrance of their temporary shelter, his own arm aching still. The bullet had not only grazed his skin but his muscle also. It could have been worse. He only hoped he could continue to use his arm effectively, at least until they got to town.

"Are we going to explore the woods some more, Mommy?"

Rachel glanced up at Jack. He could see the weariness in her expression as she answered. "We will, honey. We're just taking a little rest. You'll have plenty of chances to use your superpowers later."

"You've been a really big boy, Aidan," Jack said. "I'm proud of you."

The boy's face glowed.

Jack glanced out at the woods surrounding them. He wondered where Denton was. He prayed he was okay. Jack had yet to hear any telltale signs coming from the woods, which made him think that Denton was still laying low and on the lookout.

Then he heard a gunshot, followed by a moan.

TWENTY

"What was that?" Rachel asked, clutching Aidan to her.

Jack rose to his feet and pulled out his gun. "I'm not sure."

"Is Denton okay?"

"I hope so."

Jack didn't fool her. She could see the worry in his eyes, in tight lines on his face, in the way he held his gun poised to fire.

Rachel waited. Minutes felt like hours. Had Apaka killed Denton? Were they coming for them now?

Denton's face flashed in her mind. *Not Denton, Lord. Keep him safe. Please.*

A moment later, Jack stepped away. Was he about to go into battle? What did he see?

"Denton," he muttered. "What happened?"

Thank You, Lord.

Denton staggered into sight, gasping as if out of breath. Smudges of dirt marked his face and his pant leg was torn. He shook his head and then smiled. "I got them. All of them. I think we're safe to keep going."

"Good work." Jack patted him on the back. "How many?"

"Four."

"Are you sure there are no more?"

"I'm fairly certain."

Jack glanced back at them. "Are you ready to keep moving? I'd like to be out of the forest before sunset."

Rachel nodded and turned to Aidan. "Are you ready to be invisible again?"

Finally, the danger seemed to be behind them. At least that's what Rachel told herself. She hadn't seen anything suspicious or been pushed to the ground for fear of losing her life in the past two hours. Perhaps Denton really had taken down all of the operatives.

"How much longer?" Aidan asked.

"Not much longer, Aidan." She hoped that was the truth. The woods seemed endless, though. She hadn't seen a car or a road or a building since they began their trek through these foothills.

"We should be close to town now. We'll get a car there and keep moving."

Rachel nodded. In other words, they'd keeping running.

How much more could she take? Her foot tangled in a vine and she hurled forward. Jack paused and grasped her arm. "Are you okay?"

She nodded, fighting tears. "I think I may have sprained my ankle. I don't know."

Jack looked up at Denton. "Here's what I want you to do. Go into town and get a vehicle for us—buy it, rent it, I don't care. We'll be waiting on the side of the road for you. Call my cell phone when you're coming. You'll make much better time without us with you. Besides, it's going to take a while for us to get to the street."

"Got it." Denton hurried off into the woods.

"I'm sorry, Jack."

He set Aidan down and bent down beside her. "Don't be sorry, Rachel. None of this is your fault."

"Or is it all my fault?"

He gave her a stern glance. "You know better than that." He felt around her ankle. "Nothing's broken."

She wiped her cheek, hating how emotional she was getting, especially in front of Aidan. "Can you help me stand?"

He nodded and took her hands into his. Gently, he pulled her to her feet. She put some weight on her ankle and cringed at the pain that ripped through her. Jack lowered her back to the ground. "It's definitely sprained."

"Let's sit and rest for a moment."

She wiped her cheeks again. "No, we need to move. To keep going. What if there are more men out there?"

"We can take a moment."

"Mommy?"

She looked down and saw Aidan's big eyes assessing her. She saw fear in their depths. "Yes, honey?"

"Are the bad guys still following us?"

Rachel brushed his hair out of his eyes. "I think we lost them."

"The good guys always win, right?"

She forced a smile. "Right. The good guys always win."

Aidan seemed satisfied with her answer. He found a stick and began an imaginary sword fight with a tree. Rachel smiled and wiped away the last of her tears…for now.

"Jack, how did they find us?"

"I wish I knew. I suppose they could have slipped a tracking device into something of ours. Maybe even the SUV."

"And the coloring book? How did that picture get there? It just doesn't make any sense."

"Believe me, I'm going to get to the bottom of this. I want answers just as much as you do."

Rachel tried to remember who had given the book to Aidan. It had been Denton. He brought the book back from the store, along with some food that first night they were here. Could someone have gotten the book between the time

Denton bought it and the time he brought it inside? It didn't seem likely. But that only left Denton...

She straightened. Could Denton be one of the bad guys? She found it hard to believe. He seemed so upright and trust-worthy with his steady gaze. Besides, Jack trusted him. That said a lot.

But Denton would have had the opportunity to write the message in the coloring book. He could have messed with her purse at Eyes headquarters or even have snuck into her room that night. He could have told Apaka where they were staying.

"Jack?"

He glanced back at her. He looked pale, like he was losing too much blood. Her heart panged at the sight.

"What is it, Rachel?"

"What if Denton has been behind these attacks? He has the means and opportunity."

He shook his head, his neck muscles straining. "It's not Denton. I'd stake my life on it."

"But—"

"Just trust me on this one, Rachel."

She leaned back against a tree. Trust him. There was a concept. One that wasn't easy to come by, especially when her life was on the line. But Jack had proven himself trust-worthy. She'd try to trust him on this also.

Jack's cell phone rang and he quickly answered. "Denton, what's going on?"

When he hung up, Rachel waited for him to explain.

"He's got a car already. He's on his way to pick us up. We're not that far from the road, he said. He'll be driving a burgundy station wagon. We'll wait at the edge of the woods until we see it."

Rachel nodded.

"Are you going to be okay to walk on that ankle?"

She nodded again. If Jack could carry Aidan around with a bullet wound, certainly she could make herself hobble to safety. But as soon as she stood up and felt the pain twist through her, she doubted her bravado.

"Come on. I can help." Jack slipped his arm around her.

Rachel swallowed, her throat dry at Jack's nearness. Why did she have to be so attracted to him? And not just physically, either. He seemed to have all of the traits that she admired in a man—loyalty, honesty, a good work ethic. Of course, he worked in a dangerous job. She never wanted to marry someone who could die in the line of duty again. At least, that's what her logic said. Why did her heart seem to feel differently?

"Aidan, do you think you could walk beside us?" Jack asked.

He nodded, now using his "sword" as a walking stick. He seemed grateful for the chance to get some liveliness out. The boy never seemed to run out of energy.

They slowly crept forward. Eventually, the sound of passing cars mixed in with the background noise of the forest. The closer they got, the more Jack slowed. Finally, Jack called Denton and, before long, a burgundy station wagon pulled off the road not far away.

As they climbed into the car, Rachel couldn't stop thinking about Denton. What if he were the insider? What if they were playing right into his hands?

Denton couldn't possibly be responsible for any of this. Jack had known the man since he was a SEAL. Jack considered himself a good judge of character. He couldn't be this horribly wrong…could he?

But who else could have drawn that picture in Aidan's coloring book? Jack had sent Denton to the store. Who else could have gotten their hands on that book in the interim period between Denton buying the book and bringing it to the house?

He glanced in the backseat. Rachel appeared to be snoozing. His arm throbbed but he'd be okay. He'd get it looked at first thing when he arrived at their destination.

"How'd that drawing get in the book, Denton? What's your theory?"

"I've been trying to figure it out also, Jack."

"Replay what happened the day you bought it."

"I picked it up at the local Walmart, along with some food and drinks. I took all of those things back to the car and then went to another store across the parking lot to pick up a sandwich. I was gone probably forty-five minutes."

"Long enough for someone to draw that picture, I suppose." Jack rubbed his chin, trying to put the pieces together.

"I guess. But how did they know where we were?"

"If I had more time, I would have checked the SUV for a tracking device. It's the only thing I can think of that makes sense. I can't believe that someone was in the house with us at Eyes. We monitored the entire property nonstop. To get inside the house would have been next to impossible."

At that moment, his cell phone rang again. He saw from the caller ID that it was Luke and decided to answer.

"What's going on?"

"I think I found our insider."

Jack sucked in a breath, waiting to hear who would be revealed. "Go on."

"Simon."

"Simon? What did you find on him?"

"I found some equipment that indicates he put a tracking device in Rachel's phone. I think he was also the one who snuck into her room that night. I think he's been giving information to Apaka."

"Does he have any connections to them? Any motive?"

"We're still looking into that."

"Where is Simon now?"

"That's the other thing. He appears to have disappeared. No one's seen him since the day you left."

Jack had checked out Simon himself before he hired him, and then again when he assigned him to guard Rachel's room. Nothing had stood out. Simon had spent six years right out of high school as the bright shining star of a metropolitan police department. He'd been an honor graduate, won awards with the police department and had always been aboveboard. Could Simon really be in the insider?

"Find him."

"I'm on it." Luke paused. "How's everything going there?"

Jack decided that the only people who would learn what had happened would be the people in this car. "Just fine. Thanks for all of your help there."

Jack hung up and told Denton what Luke had told him.

"Why would Simon be working for Apaka?"

"That's my question. Luke is looking into it."

"Maybe we'll get some answers soon."

Jack stared at the road before them, that was now cloaked with darkness. He clenched his jaw. He had a feeling the worst was yet to come.

TWENTY-ONE

When Rachel awoke, the sun's muted morning rays were just beginning to peek over the horizon. She blinked a couple of times, trying to figure out where she was. An old farmhouse stood in front of her and a barn, woods, and cornfields beyond that. In the distance, an older man and woman stepped from the white clapboard house to greet them. Even from where Rachel sat, she could see from their gait that they were surprised to have company.

Rachel sat up in her seat and pushed her hair back from her face, trying to look halfway presentable, at least. Aidan still dozed in the seat beside her. Had last night been a nightmare? She looked at her legs and saw the scratches and bruises there from their desperate escape. No, it definitely hadn't been a nightmare.

Jack turned around from the front seat, exhaustion showing in his eyes. "We're here."

Rachel blinked as she tried to comprehend the new surroundings. She, at the moment, couldn't even remember how long they'd been on the road or in what direction they'd been headed. "Where's here?"

Jack smiled. "You'll see. Hop on out and I'll introduce you."

She slipped from the car, stepping tentatively on her ankle. She winced with pain and leaned against the car for balance for a moment. Jack rounded the vehicle just as the older couple reached them.

"Rachel, I'd like for you to meet my mom and dad."

Rachel's eyes widened, her pain temporarily forgotten. "Your mom and dad? Wow." She extended her hand. "It's nice to meet you."

"You, too, Rachel, though this is all quite a surprise." Mrs. Sergeant's eyes went to Jack's shirt. Blood covered his sleeve and a makeshift bandage had been tied around his biceps where he'd been shot. "What happened, son? You're hurt."

Jack looked down at his arm and shrugged. "It's nothing. Just a little scratch."

"It's hardly a scratch. He needs to have the wound treated ASAP." Rachel gave Jack a pointed look. He was so busy watching out for everyone else that someone had to watch out for him. Rachel accepted the position…for now. How could she not? The man had saved her life more times than she could count.

Mrs. Sergeant, a petite woman in her sixties with short, straight hair, nodded in agreement. "I can fix that as soon as we get inside." She looked beyond Jack and smiled warmly. "Denton, good to see you again, despite whatever circumstances might have brought you this way. Who's the little guy in the backseat?"

Rachel placed a hand on Aidan's leg. "This is my son, Aidan."

"It's always good to have children around here. Doesn't happen often enough." Mrs. Sergeant waved her hand in a circle and stepped toward the house. "Come on inside. I'll get you something to eat, and, Jack, I'll get you sewed up. Then you can explain what this visit is about. I have a feeling it isn't because you're homesick for your old Mom and Pops."

Rachel tried to take a step forward but stopped as pain coursed through her. She reached for something to hold on to.

Aidan's big, saucer-like brown eyes locked on her. "Mommy? What's wrong?"

"My ankle's just a little sore. Mommy twisted it last night."

Jack slipped an arm around her waist. "Let me help."

His proximity sent shivers through her. She wished getting rid of her feelings for him was as easy as turning a switch on and off. Instead, her feelings felt more like the Apaka operatives who were chasing them—like something she'd never be able to lose.

Inside the cozy home, Mrs. Sergeant propped Rachel up in a recliner and placed an ice pack on her ankle. Then she turned to Jack and stared at his blood-soaked shirt. Rachel could only imagine how seeing that much blood on her son made her fcel. Rachel knew how she'd feel if it had been Aidan hurt—no matter his age.

"Are you sure you don't want to go to the doctor, son?" Mrs. Sergeant removed the cloth around Jack's biceps.

"I'm fine," Jack said. "I'm sure you'll do a better job than they would anyway."

"He was always getting hurt as a youngster," Mrs. Sergeant said, pulling out some antibiotic. "He always had this adventurous spirit that ended up getting him in trouble. Not serious trouble. Just some broken bones, cuts and scrapes. In other words, he was all boy."

Rachel smiled. That seemed to describe Aidan pretty accurately also. Rachel always said that God gave her a boy to toughen her up, because Aidan was so often fearless and daredevilish.

Aidan climbed into her lap at that moment, his demeanor showing that he soaked everything in. "Do the bad guys know we're here, Mr. Jack?"

Jack and Rachel exchanged a look, while Mrs. Sergeant raised her eyebrows in obvious curiosity. Jack winced as his mother poured some hydrogen peroxide on his wound. "No,

Aidan. We're safe for now. You don't have to pretend to be invisible for a while yet. Have I told you yet what a great job you did with that yesterday?"

Aidan nodded, his eyes beaming with pride.

"Do I even want to hear this story?" Mrs. Sergeant shook her head.

"Probably not."

She placed some bandages over the wound and patted her son's arm. "That's just fine with me. How about if I fix everyone some breakfast instead?"

Breakfast sounded perfect to Rachel. Just the mention of it caused her stomach to rumble. Aidan scurried into the kitchen after Mrs. Sergeant, asking if he could help her cook. Rachel took the opportunity to close her eyes for a moment.

She liked the feeling of Jack's childhood home. That's exactly what it felt like—a home. It exuded warmth and love and memories. For a moment, her heart longed for her own childhood home. Being there meant nothing without her mom and dad, though. It just brought back sad memories of their early passing.

Breakfast consisted of biscuits and gravy, eggs and bacon. Better yet, it was full of lighthearted conversation. Jack's parents obviously knew Denton and practically treated him like a son. Rachel mostly stayed quiet and let everyone else do the talking. She tried to forget the events of the past week and pretend everything was normal, but she couldn't.

She knew it was only a matter of time before Apaka found them here. Then they'd be on the run again. Where would they go next? When would they ever stop? Would she ever have a home like this one where she felt safe and loved again?

Rachel looked away from the food she pushed around the plate and saw Jack studying her. She tried to smile and reassure him she was fine, but she couldn't. Instead, she cleared her throat and pushed her plate back, her appetite gone. "Would it be okay if I got cleaned up? I think a shower would do wonders for me right now."

"I'll keep an eye on Aidan," Jack said, his gaze still on her. "The bathroom's right down the hallway."

Mrs. Sergeant rose. "Let me pull out a few things for you."

Rachel hobbled to the shower and gratefully accepted the sweatpants and T-shirt that Mrs. Sergeant offered. She wished she could wash away her problems like she washed away the dirt covering her. The grit reminded her again of their narrow escape.

After her shower, she pulled on the clothes Mrs. Sergeant had left for her and opened the bathroom door, watching as steam invaded the hallway. Her ankle was feeling a little better now, and she could put a little weight on it. She began her hobble through the hallway back to the family room. She paused around the corner when she heard Aidan's voice drifting across the house.

"Mr. Jack?"

"Yes, Aidan?"

"I don't want you to leave. Ever. I like you."

Rachel leaned against the wall, her heart nearly pounding through her chest. She held her breath, waiting for Jack's response.

"I've really liked getting to know you better, too, Aidan." Jack's voice sounded full of warmth. "We've had a lot of fun together, haven't we? Going fishing, playing superheroes?"

Tears popped to Rachel's eyes. She'd thought about how she would feel when Jack was no longer a part of her life. She'd be devastated. But Aidan had become more attached than she'd realized. He'd begun looking at Jack like the father figure he longed for.

Rachel should have been more careful. She should have seen this coming, should have protected her son more and tried to prevent him from becoming attached.

"Will you teach me to play baseball one day? When I get back to my house? I even have a bat. Mommy isn't very good at sports."

"Oh, she's not? I thought your mom was good at anything she wanted to be good at."

Rachel could hear the tease in Jack's voice.

"I'd love to teach you to play baseball one day, little man. Baseball used to be one of my favorite sports when I was growing up."

"Mr. Jack?"

"Yes, Aidan?"

"I love you."

"I love you, too, Aidan."

Rachel closed her eyes and let her chin drop to her chest in dismay. Her heart felt warmed by the possibility that Jack could possibly be there for Aidan, and wary that perhaps he was making empty promises.

Jack had made it clear that he was just doing his job. The feelings that she thought Jack had for her—that she'd thought she'd seen in his eyes—were all wrong. That meant that when this was all over, Jack would be out of their lives. It was for the best, she reminded herself. Rachel didn't want to ever get involved with someone with Jack's job description again. She wanted someone whom she didn't have to worry about getting killed on the job.

She stepped around the corner and spotted Jack and Aidan playing a game on his smartphone on the floor. She cleared her throat. "Aidan."

Her son looked up just as Jack saw her and stood. The way he stepped forward made her think he wanted to talk. Not now. She needed space right now.

"I just beat Mr. Jack at another game of Tic Tac Toe on his phone," Aidan announced proudly.

Rachel smiled. "Come on. We need to get you changed. Let's give Mr. Jack some time alone."

"But I'm not finished with the game yet!"

"We'll finish it later. Come on. You need to hop in the bath." She glanced up at Jack and hoped her look made it loud and clear that she didn't appreciate empty promises.

Jack could tell from the glare Rachel gave him that she'd overheard the conversation Aidan had brought up. His heart plunged.

He'd meant the things he told Aidan. Aidan was such a good kid, and Jack could so easily picture himself helping the boy learn how to play baseball or to catch a football. More than picturing it, Jack knew that he wanted to do those things. He wanted to be there for Aidan...and for Rachel.

As Aidan scurried away, Jack started to stop him, to ask Rachel if they could talk. But it was obvious she wasn't in the mood right now. Besides, he had to touch base with Luke and to formulate his next move. His parents had cleared out of the house to give them some space. His mom had left for town to buy some supplies, and his dad had escaped outside to do some work. Meanwhile, Denton had set up base in the dining room and was busy playing catchup after their escape yesterday.

He joined Denton at an old laptop that Jack's dad let them use.

"I just talked to the FBI. They're searching the vice admiral's house right now for clues. All the bodies were gone when they got there, however."

"Gone?"

"Someone took time to clean up."

Jack rubbed his chin. If the FBI could have ID'd those men, it might have led the authorities to their cell. Whoever was behind this plot knew what they were doing. They were smart. They'd figure out Rachel and Aidan were here in a matter of days, if not less.

He had to come up with his next plan of action. He had a feeling that the days of Apaka toying with them were over. When they found Rachel again, there would be a straight-out attack, no holds barred. Jack had to figure out a way to keep them safe, whatever the cost.

Just then, Jack's cell phone buzzed. He looked down at the number and saw that it was the vice admiral. He braced himself for the upcoming conversation.

"Jack, where are you?"

"Apaka found us at your residence, sir. We had to escape. We're at a safe location—for now. I don't plan on staying in any one place too long, however."

"How are Rachel and Aidan?"

"Shaken and scared, but okay."

"Any idea how they found you?"

"We're looking into it now, sir. One of the guards at Eyes is missing. We believe he may have been working for Apaka. Luke is searching for him now. We believe he may have been the inside leak and that he planted a tracking device in the cell phone I gave to Rachel."

"We got another letter addressed to Rachel."

Jack tensed. "What did it say?"

"It said, 'You can run, but you can't hide.' It had the same powdery substance inside, so of course we had to have it tested for anthrax. It was clear. Just a hoax. But I have a feeling the threat behind it isn't."

"I plan on keeping Rachel and Aidan safe, sir. I'm willing to give my life if I have to. We're hoping that once Simon is found we'll get some answers."

"You realize that Apaka is probably on the trail to you now."

"I'm just going to let Rachel and Aidan rest for a bit. Then we're gone again, sir."

"Keep me updated."

Jack hung up just in time to spot Rachel standing in the doorway, her eyes as big as saucers. "What's going on?" she asked.

Before he could answer, his cell phone buzzed again. Luke. He held up a finger to Rachel, asking her to wait. He'd been trying to get in touch with Luke all morning.

"You're not going to like this," Luke started.

"What is it?"

"We found Simon."

"And?"

"He's dead."

TWENTY-TWO

Rachel stared at Jack, trying to read his expression. It was pointless. Rachel wondered if part of his training was on how to be absolutely unreadable. As soon as he hung up, she raised her eyebrows. "Is everything okay?"

"They found Simon."

"That's good news. Maybe Luke can get some information out of him that will point to the people behind these threats."

Jack shook his head. "He's dead."

Rachel gasped. "Dead? What happened?"

"He was found shot in the head not far from the Eyes headquarters."

"Poor Simon." Rachel's hand flew over her mouth. "I guess I shouldn't say poor Simon. He tried to kill me...didn't he?" She shook her head, nothing making sense at the moment.

"We're still trying to put the pieces together."

She shook her head again, the puzzle pieces were on the precipice of fitting. She sighed and leaned against the doorpost. She'd temporarily forgotten about how upset she was with Jack. There were more important matters at hand, at the moment.

Was there even a connection between the people on the list? Why was it taking so long to discover it? Maybe this was all just one big game that Apaka was playing with them.

"Rachel…"

She looked up and saw that earnest look in Jack's eyes. It started to melt her heart, as it always did. But she had to think about Aidan.

"Please don't make promises to my son that you can't keep, Jack."

"I intend to keep them, Rachel."

"So what you're telling me is that once this is all over you're going to take little breaks from your high-stress job with Eyes so that you can come over to our place and throw around a baseball?"

"I would like to do that, Rachel. I'd like to be there for Aidan."

"I don't think you understand, Jack." She leaned toward him. "Aidan wants a dad. It's great that you think you're going to be a part of his life when this is all done, but we both know the truth, don't we?"

"What truth is that, Rachel?"

"The truth that you're just doing your job. The truth that crazy circumstances have pulled us all together and maybe made us all feel an attachment to each other. The truth is that that attachment is just an illusion. If we survive this, life will return as normal. You'll move on to your next assignment. And Aidan and I will go back to being a fatherless child and a widow."

"Rachel, it's not—"

Just then, the back door swung open and Aidan came running in. "Mommy! Mr. Jack! Look! Mr. Sergeant made me a sword out of wood!" He swashed it around in the air. "Isn't it cool?"

Rachel forced a smile, but her heart plunged. Jack hadn't been able to respond, but that was okay, she told herself. She simply needed to distance herself from him now more than ever. If not for her heart's sake, then for her son's.

* * *

Rachel sat on the porch with some coffee and watched Aidan sword-fighting with imaginary bad guys. She couldn't get the conversation with Jack out of her mind, so instead she turned her thoughts over to the list. She repeated the names and the career titles like she had so many times before.

A farmer, an engineer, a scientist.

An entomologist, a professor, a nonprofit director.

She shook her head. Nothing made sense still. She needed to accept the fact that it might never make sense. That she might never feel safe again.

The front door squeaked open beside her. She braced herself, half hoping to see Jack, half hoping not to see Jack.

Instead, she spotted Mrs. Sergeant. "You mind if I join you?"

Rachel smiled. "Not at all. I'd love it, actually."

Mrs. Sergeant lowered herself into the rocking chair beside Rachel. They rocked silently for a moment, each seeming to enjoy the peace that surrounded the farm. Rachel only hoped that that peace wasn't just a facade.

"Jack tells me your husband died over in Afghanistan."

Rachel nodded and took another sip of coffee. "He did. Right before Aidan was born. It wasn't exactly the way I envisioned my future, but you work with what you've got."

"It seems like you've done a good job with what you've got. Aidan is precious."

Rachel smiled and watched Aidan tumble on the grass in an imaginary battle. "He is. He's been a real gift. It hasn't always been easy being a single mom, but I couldn't ask for a better kid."

"I was a single mother for a while. I understand how hard it can be."

Her head swung toward Mrs. Sergeant in surprise. "You were? Jack didn't tell me…"

"It was before Jack was born. My first husband was killed

in an auto accident when Jack's older brother was only two months old. It was devastating. I never thought I'd fall in love again."

"But you did."

"I did. I was determined to stay single rather than marry the wrong man. I only wanted the best for my son. That's a mom's job, after all, to watch out for her kids."

"I agree."

"But then I found Ike."

Rachel thought about Jack's dad. He shared a lot of Jack's qualities. "You guys seem like a good match."

"We are." Mrs. Sergeant turned to Rachel. "I'm usually not one to mince words too much, Rachel, yet here I am beating around the bush. I can tell my son cares about you."

Rachel sucked in a breath. How did she even approach this conversation? The only way she knew how: with honesty. "I'm not so sure about that, Mrs. Sergeant."

"I'm quite certain. I'm also quite certain that he feels a lot of guilt over his failed marriage to Jennifer. The military can be so hard on families."

"It can be. I know that I can't ever become involved with a military man. I want a stable life for Aidan. I want a husband who will come home every night. I don't want to lose someone else that I love." Did she just say the *L* word? Did she love Jack?

Mrs. Sergeant turned toward her. "Love always requires risk, my dear. There are no guarantees in life. I never thought I would lose a husband to a drunk driver. But sometimes things are out of our hands—whatever career you choose."

Rachel couldn't argue with that. After all, she was a nonprofit director who was being hunted by terrorists.

Mrs. Sergeant patted her hand. "I know I sound biased. I am biased. But I've seen the way both of you look at each other. And I know my son. He's stubborn. So even though he would be very unhappy with me if he knew I was having this conversation, I felt like I should anyway."

"I appreciate your honesty, Mrs. Sergeant."

She stood. "Now that I've meddled, I better get started on dinner. I'm not used to having four extra mouths to feed, but I love every minute of it. Nothing better than having family and loved ones close."

Having family was great. Rachel had once had dreams of a big family. She'd learned to be content with what she had.

Until Jack Sergeant came along.

Rachel frowned. She had to stop thinking about him. It didn't matter if his mother thought he cared about her. Rachel had to guard her heart.

Mrs. Sergeant retreated back inside, leaving Rachel alone with her thoughts.

Stop thinking about him, she chided herself.

She glanced at Aidan instead. He'd given up his sword fight in favor of chasing a butterfly. She smiled. She would love to be a carefree child again.

Her gaze traveled across the road to the cornfields. She scanned the rows of stalks for any sign of trouble. She'd become accustomed to doing just that—being on guard wherever she was, whatever she was doing.

She needed to be equally as on guard when it came to her heart and Jack Sergeant.

The cornstalks danced in the breeze.

Think about the list, Rachel, not Jack.

A farmer, an engineer, a scientist.

An entomologist, a professor, a nonprofit director.

She watched the cornstalks, mulling over her thoughts. How could the people on that list possibly be connected? What was she missing?

She sat up straight.

She knew the connection between the people on the list.

TWENTY-THREE

Jack straightened and stretched his back. They'd managed to retrieve some video images from the vice admiral's house thanks to a server the images had been saved onto at Eyes. But studying the feeds for the past hour had proven useless. They could find no clues from their time at Vice Admiral Harris's home. Nothing that would lead them to the answers they so desperately needed.

"Jack!" Rachel appeared in the doorway, breathless and shaken.

Adrenaline rushed through him at the sight of her. "What's wrong?"

"I think I know the connection between the people on the list, Jack."

Jack's heart sped a bit. "Go on."

She gulped in another breath. "I know this might sound crazy, but I think the connection might be my parents."

"Why would you think that?"

"Just think about it. A farmer, a scientist, an entomologist, a political science professor, and an engineer. Bring all of those people together, and what could they be working on? Something for the Department of Agriculture. Farming, crops, fertilizer. Agroterrorism."

"Agroterrorism?" He rubbed his chin and glanced at Denton. "We never considered that angle. But you're right.

It does make sense. The terrorists might want information that could destroy our food supply."

"That photo that was stolen from my house? It was from a cookout at my parents' house, right? What if the person behind these attacks was in that photo? What if he'd been at my parents' house for that cookout, and he remembered the photo, and he was afraid we might find it and realize it was him?"

Jack rushed to the computer. "I think you're on to something, Rachel."

"The only thing I can't figure out is why they'd target people connected with my parents when they're dead. Maybe all of the people on the list worked on a project for the Department of Agriculture together, and Apaka wanted information from them. I don't know. And I don't know how I'm connected other than my parents."

Jack placed his hands on either side of her arms to steady her. "You did great, Rachel. Let Denton and I take over now. We'll see what we can find out."

She nodded, still looking dazed and breathless. She started to walk away but stopped. "Jack?"

"Yes?"

"Maybe there is hope."

"There's always hope, Rachel."

Jack hung up the phone. He'd just talked to the son of the Kansas wheat farmer who'd been killed. The son confirmed that his father had been a consultant once for the Department of Agriculture. He estimated it was probably five years ago.

Jack felt sure that Rachel was dead on with her suspicions. Her parents were the connection. Why hadn't he seen it earlier? Now they just had to figure out why. He'd put in calls to the families of the others on the list, as well. It the meantime, it was a waiting game until he heard back from them.

Denton leaned back in his chair, casually putting his hands behind his head. "Should we call the Department of Agriculture?"

Jack took another sip of coffee, surviving at the moment on coffee and adrenaline. "They won't tell us anything. The vice admiral would have more luck with that, but I'm not ready to present this theory to him yet, not until we have something solid to back it up."

Denton sat up and ran a hand over his five o'clock shadow, appearing equally as exhausted as Jack felt. "What if her parents were working on a top-secret project for the Department of Agriculture? What if it's not even on the books? Maybe they were even working for the other side."

Jack considered the idea for a moment.

"They wouldn't do that," someone said from the hallway. "They were good people."

Jack jerked his head up and spotted Rachel in the doorway. She didn't wait for an invitation. She walked into the room and pulled out an extra chair around the dining room table. The way she sat down made it clear she planned on staying. "Aidan is making cupcakes with your mom. I want to help."

"I'm not sure what you can do, Rachel," Jack started.

"For starters, I can assure you that my parents would never work for the other side. They were good people. They loved their country." Her eyes showed stubborn determination.

"We have to examine every possibility, Rachel," Jack said. "As painful as it might be."

"Here's the bigger question. Let's say they were working on a project—authorized or unauthorized—for the Department of Agriculture. Let's say all the people on the list did help them with it in some way. The fact is that I didn't help them and my name was on the list also. Why would my name be there? That's the only thing that doesn't make sense about my theory."

"Maybe you did help, you just didn't know it." Denton shrugged at the suggestion. "Maybe they tested out a project on you."

Rachel narrowed her eyes at Denton. "Now you sound like Aidan, who's watched way too many superhero movies. My parents would never 'test out a project' on me."

Jack leaned toward her. "Maybe it was something subtle, that doesn't even seem suspicious. Did they grow a garden in your backyard? Tell you anything about a fertilizer or genetically modified fruit or vegetable?"

She shook her head. "They never brought their work home with them. I wish...I wish there was something I could tell you. I want this to end more than anyone. I feel like the answers are right within our grasp."

"They are, Rachel. We're waiting on some phone calls. We need to confirm this theory and then we can start putting some pieces together."

"I just can't imagine my parents having any affiliation with terrorists or why Apaka would be hunting people down now, after my parents have been dead for four years." She leaned back in her chair. "We may have one answer, but now, at the same time, I have a lot more questions."

Jack could see the anguish on her face. He wanted nothing more than to pull her into his arms and comfort her. He didn't, though.

"There's one big question that's haunting me," Rachel practically whispered.

"What's that?"

"What if my parents' accident wasn't an accident at all?"

Rachel couldn't stop thinking about her parents now. They were the connection. She felt sure of it. But she also knew there was very little she could do except try to be "normal" for Aidan.

While Rachel had brainstormed with Jack and Denton, Aidan had made cupcakes with Jack's mom, gone fishing with Jack's dad and been cared for by two adults who obviously adored children.

Rachel's heart felt that familiar ache. She longed for Aidan to have grandparents who'd spoil him and let him have weekend sleepovers and sneak him candy when he wasn't allowed.

All Aidan wanted now was to watch a movie. Jack's parents and Denton had all opted out and gone to bed early. Rachel would have also, except that Aidan was so adamant about watching the movie. The boy deserved an evening of fun after everything they'd been through. The problem was that he'd begged Jack to stay and watch the movie also. Jack had said yes.

Rachel glanced across the couch. Her heart lurched when she saw that Aidan had fallen asleep in Jack's arms. His head seemed to fit perfectly under Jack's chin, and Jack's strong arms held him up. Lights from the TV flickered across their faces and the half-eaten bowl of popcorn rested on the table in front of them.

For a moment, Rachel felt like a family.

But they weren't, she reminded herself.

This whole situation had thrown her emotions into an upheaval. Jack was simply doing his job. Somehow, it had begun to feel like so much more than that to her, though. How had she let her emotions get so out of control?

But Jack had been so good for Aidan…so good for her, too, if she were to really think about it. How did he feel? The same way?

No, it was just his job.

She looked away, down at her hands, before Jack saw the truth in her gaze.

Soon, they'd return to their normal life…she hoped, at

least. That life would be absent of Jack. Why did the thought of that cause her heart to ache with sadness?

"How about if I go put him to bed?" Jack whispered.

Rachel nodded, her throat burning with emotions. "I'll go turn down the sheets."

Quietly, they walked down the hallway. Rachel opened the door to Aidan's room and quickly scanned the space, as she'd become in the habit of doing. Nothing appeared out of place. Rachel pulled the covers back and stepped away as Jack gently placed Aidan there and tucked him in.

Unwillingly, tears sprang to her eyes. She'd always known she'd wanted a father for Aidan, but those desires hit her now a hundredfold.

When Jack stepped back, Rachel leaned down to kiss Aidan's forehead before quietly scooting out of the room. She tried to walk away before Jack caught a glimpse of her face, but it was too late. He grabbed her arm and she turned to face him. She saw the questions in his gaze.

"Rachel?"

She froze. "Yes?"

"You're more than an assignment to me."

She blinked a few times as his words sank in. "I'm sorry. What was that?"

He stepped closer, his eyes sucking her into something that felt close to a trance. "I know I said I was just doing my job, Rachel, but the truth is, I can't imagine my life without you or Aidan. There are a million reasons why we shouldn't be together. I've thought about all of them."

"And?"

"I've realized there are a million reasons why we should be together also. I know you don't ever want to date a military man again, though."

That was what she'd said, wasn't it? Could she date someone with Jack's job description? In her heart, she already knew the answer. "Someone very wise just told me today that love always requires risks, no matter what the job."

He tucked a hair behind her ear and cupped her cheek with his hand. "The more I get to know you, the more I realize that you and Aidan make my life feel complete. I haven't known you that long, but I already can't imagine a life without you."

Rachel sucked in a breath, her limbs quivering in sync with her stomach. Her heart soared. Jack felt the same way about her as she felt about him. If nothing else good had come from this whole situation, there was that. There was the fact that she finally felt ready to take a risk.

"Are you ready to stop beating yourself up over your ex-wife leaving you? You have to know that she's the one who walked away. I know marriage is a two-way street, but it sounds like you did everything you could to make it work. You have to stop blaming yourself for it."

He lowered his head, and Rachel laid a hand on his chest. She held her breath, waiting for him to respond, waiting to see his eyes.

"Jack?"

He opened his eyes and Rachel saw something new there. Hope maybe?

"Thank you, Rachel. Hearing you say that makes me feel like a weight has been lifted from my shoulders."

"God's the one who can lift all of our burdens, Jack. Just give them to Him."

"You're incredible, Rachel. You do know that, don't you?"

"I just think that God takes the bad things in our lives and turns them into something beautiful. If Andrew hadn't been killed, I would have never started Operation 26 Letters. If you hadn't been through the things you've been through, you probably wouldn't have started Eyes. God can take tragedies and turn them into ministries."

"Rachel..."

"Yes?"

He leaned down until his lips brushed hers. Her arms encircled his neck as they pulled closer together.

As quickly as the kiss began, Jack pulled away. Rachel stepped back, confused. What had just happened? She looked up and saw the anguish drawn on the tight lines on Jack's face.

"What am I doing?" He ran a hand over his face, his voice husky with burden.

"I don't understand…"

"Rachel." He closed his eyes and shook his head. "I can't do this."

"But you just said—"

"I know. I know what I said. But…but Rachel." His eyes met hers again, and Rachel saw the anguish there. "Rachel, I have to stop pretending. I have to own up to something."

"What's that?"

"Rachel, I'm the reason Andrew died."

TWENTY-FOUR

Rachel took a step back. Her chest suddenly felt tight, like she couldn't catch her breath.

Had she just heard Jack correctly? Her eyebrows drew together in confusion as her thoughts began a collision course with her emotions. "What do you mean, Jack? I don't understand."

Jack winced, the rigid set of his shoulders making him appear like he carried the weight of the world. "I didn't want to tell you. I thought…I guess I thought I could just keep it to myself, that you didn't ever have to know. But I care about you too much. I have to come clean about what happened that night Andrew died."

Rachel suddenly felt like she could throw up, as if an ominous cloud had appeared and she needed to brace herself for the coming storm. She ran her hands over her face, trying to gain some composure. "Okay."

"Let's go sit in the living room. Is that okay?"

She nodded and followed Jack into the other room. They both sat stiffly across from each other on the couch. Jack pulled his eyes up to meet hers, and Rachel could see the pain in their depths.

"Rachel, I was sent over to Afghanistan by the CIA to work undercover. My assignment was to keep an eye on your husband."

"On Andrew? Why?"

"We were afraid he was selling secrets to the other side. There had been a large number of battles we'd gone into where the enemy seemed to know our plans and prepare in advance for us. So many good men were killed in those ambushes. We had to find out who the leak was. Everything pointed to Andrew."

"Why? Why would things point to Andrew? What had he done?"

Jack sucked in a long breath and looked in the distance before meeting Rachel's gaze again. "He'd disappear from base for large chunks of unaccounted time. People said that they'd seen him fraternizing with the enemy on those excursions. Nothing could be proven. None of the guys on his SEALs team wanted to give him up. They're more loyal to each other than brothers. So they stationed me at the base, posing as a Joint Forces Command liaison." He looked at his hands. "I already told you that I worked with him. I didn't tell you that I was stationed there to spy on him."

Rachel could hardly breathe. Her muscles tightened into knots as she waited to hear the rest of Jack's explanation. Time seemed fluid, like gelatin that she was mucking through. She leaned back, away from Jack, as she tried to process her thoughts.

"I got to know Andrew. I liked him. I really did. I thought if he wasn't my assignment, we could be friends. But I was there on assignment." He paused. "The night he died, we were supposed to go into Kabul together during some free time. But I got some last-minute intelligence that suggested he could be meeting with someone that evening. I didn't know if he would still try to have that meeting if I went with him. So I told him to go ahead without me. He wasn't going to, but I pushed him to do it just so I could follow him."

"What happened?" Even to her own ears, her words sound thin, fragile, like they could break at any moment.

"I wasn't that far behind him when his vehicle hit an improvised explosive device. I rushed over to him and pulled him out of the Hummer. He was still alive—but barely."

Rachel's throat burned as she pictured the scene, as she pictured Andrew, pictured Jack. Tears pushed to the surface.

Jack ran a hand over his face again, each action seeming weighed down by a million anchors. "Andrew knew he wasn't going to make it. He asked me to keep an eye on you. That was the last thing he said before he passed."

Rachel wiped a tear from her eyes using the edge of her sweatshirt. She crossed her arms over her chest, trying to come to terms with what Jack told her. "So, you're telling me that if you hadn't told him to go ahead into Kabul, that he wouldn't have hit that IED? He would have been safe and sound at the base. He'd still be alive right now?"

He nodded. "I'm sorry, Rachel. The whole time we thought he was selling secrets to the other side, he must have really been trying to help Meredith and her family."

Rachel's head spun, and nothing seemed to make sense. "I don't know what to say. I…I need time to process this."

"Of course." His voice sounded hoarse, raw.

Both of their heads snapped toward the doorway when they heard a noise there. Mrs. Sergeant stood there, looking back and forth between the two of them, wringing her hands together. "Rachel. Jack. Where's Aidan?"

Rachel stood, fear pumping through her veins. "What do you mean, 'Where's Aidan?' He's sleeping in his room."

Mrs. Sergeant looked ghostly pale. "I just stuck my head in there to check on him. His bed is empty."

Nausea turned in Rachel's gut. Jack appeared behind her as her legs buckled. "Aidan. Oh no, not Aidan." He lowered her back to the couch, but Rachel bounced back to her feet.

This was no time to sit down and worry. It was a time for action, to do something.

Jack raced to the front door and peered out the window atop it. "Let's not get ahead of ourselves. He could have just wandered to another part of the house."

Rachel shook her head, shock setting in. "No, they got him. I just know Apaka got him."

Jack hurried back over to her and placed a hand on her shoulder, back in soldier mode. "Mom, wake up Dad. We've got to look for Aidan. He was just there a few minutes ago. Rachel, get Denton and let him know what's going on. And then sit tight. We'll find him."

Rachel hardly heard him. She sprinted up the stairs, ignoring her aching ankle, to Aidan's room. She wanted to see for herself. Maybe he was under the bed? In the closet? Maybe he'd had a nightmare?

She threw the door open. The covers were thrown back, as if he'd flipped them off to go to the bathroom or something. First, she looked under the bed, in the closet. He wasn't in the room.

She hurried down the hall and opened the bathroom door. No one. She threw the shower curtain back. It was empty.

Jack approached down the hallway.

"He's not in his room or in here."

"I'm going to go outside and search for him. You need to stay in here."

"I can't stay in here. This is my son we're talking about. What if Apaka has gotten to him?" Her words caused ice to form in her chest.

"Denton and I will be searching outside. You need to stay safe so you can take care of him when we find him. Do you understand?" He grasped her shoulders and shook her, bringing her out of her daze.

"Jack, you have to find him," she whispered.

He nodded, confidence in his gaze. "We will."

He hurried away and Rachel stood in the hallway a moment, letting the shadows splay over her skin. Aidan. Her sweet Aidan. She sank to her knees. What if something happened to her son?

She felt an arm around her and looked up to see Jack's mom. "Come on downstairs. Jack and Denton are outside looking right now. They'll find him."

Not if Apaka already had him.

Rachel nodded. "I'll be right down. I just need a minute alone, please."

Jack's mom nodded and stepped away, giving Rachel just one more worried glance back.

Rachel stayed on her knees. Where could Aidan be? Did Apaka get him? Jack had said that Aidan was never the target, only Rachel. What if Aidan had simply wandered out to explore? He'd loved his time on the farm. Maybe he'd wanted to see more. He was only four, after all. He didn't understand the gravity of the situation.

What if he *had* just gone outside to explore? Where would he most likely be?

The barn! That had been Aidan's favorite spot. He'd even asked Rachel earlier if they could build a barn behind their house. Had Jack remembered to check the barn?

New life pulsed through her. Rachel had to go there herself. She couldn't assume that Jack would think about the barn.

Quietly, she crept down the steps. She could see Jack's parents seated on the couch, their hands knotted in front of them and lines of worry at their eyes. Careful so that they wouldn't hear her, she stepped off the staircase and darted around the corner to the back door. Her hand gripped the knob and turned slowly. She cracked the door open and slid out without a sound. As soon as she stepped foot on the grass, she began a sprint to the barn. Her ankle screamed for relief, but she pushed on anyway.

She didn't care what Jack told her. She had to help look for her son. This was her son. She couldn't sit idly by when something might be wrong. She'd never forgive herself if she could have done something to help.

The barn grew closer and closer, and her lungs burned for air, but she didn't care. She pushed ahead. Finally at the barn, she threw open the doors and stepped into the dark place.

A shudder raced through her. "Aidan?"

Nothing.

She stepped in farther. "Aidan, can you hear me, honey? Are you in here?"

She heard movement in the distance. Maybe she should have waited for Jack, she thought as fear crawled over her.

No, she had no time. She had to get her son.

She grabbed a rake from beside the door and stepped forward, toward the noise. All sounded quiet again. What had that noise been? Birds? A barn cat? Or something more sinister?

"Aidan? Is that you, honey?"

"Mom—" She heard Aidan's voice, but it sounded like it had been muted, like…a hand had gone over his mouth. Her heart lurched.

She ran toward the voice only to hear a gun cock. "Stop right there, Rachel."

She froze, still squeezing the rake in her hands.

Whose voice was that? She'd heard it before, only now it sounded more gravelly and almost had the hint of an Eastern European accent.

Her blood went ice-cold as realization washed over her. She knew exactly whose voice that was.

She lifted a prayer, knowing that the fight of her life was about to begin.

TWENTY-FIVE

Luke stepped from the shadows and into a beam of moonlight that crept in through a crack in the siding. A cocky grin stretched across his face. Rachel's heart plunged as cold fear invaded her.

"Luke? I thought you were at Eyes. When did you get here?" Even as the words left her mouth, she felt the truth sinking in. Luke wasn't supposed to be here. He was holding a gun. Pointed at her.

His eyebrow flickered toward the sky. "A few minutes ago."

Rachel drew in a ragged breath, daring to ask the next question. "Where's Aidan?"

"He's not hurt. He's just in the corner, playing by himself like a good little boy."

"Aidan?" Her gaze searched the darkness, trying—desperate—to see him through the inkiness.

"I'm right here, Mommy! I'm trying to make a sword out of this stick."

Luke nodded toward the other end of the barn, the side closest to the country lane that stretched beside the farm. "We need to move. And fast. So no arguments or—" Luke made a shooting motion with his fingers.

"Why, Luke? Why are you doing this?"

"No time to explain all of those fun details now, Rachel." He grabbed her arm. "Now walk."

Without time to think, she swung the rake until it knocked Luke in the side of the head. He toppled for a moment and grasped at his head. He righted himself and drew the gun. "That was uncalled for. You're lucky I don't shoot you now."

"Luke, put down the gun," a deep, familiar voice commanded.

Rachel gasped and turned toward the voice. Jack. Jack had found them. Praise God.

Luke shook his head and let out an agitated laugh. "Jack, just let us walk away. This is really none of your business. You've done everything in your power, up to this point."

"I'd say it is my business."

Luke sneered. "Only because you had to go and fall in love with your client. That's not advisable, boss. I think that was covered in Training 101."

Jack slowly crept closer. "Let's not talk about me right now, Luke. Let's talk about you. Why are you doing this?"

Rachel looked over in the direction that Luke had pointed. She could make out the vague outline of Aidan, sitting in the corner of the stall. If only she could get to him. But she didn't want to make any sudden moves, didn't want to risk being shot in front of her son. Yet she needed to hold him, protect him.

She looked back at Jack behind her, his calm demeanor. He was trying to keep everyone's emotions down. His gaze caught hers and Rachel saw something there. He was trying to give her some sort of message, but what?

Luke's gun was still aimed at her. All it would take was one moment for her world to forever change. She sucked in a breath.

Aidan. She just wanted to get Aidan.

"Guess what? Terrorism pays pretty well. I bet you didn't

know that I'm originally from Uzbekistan. Do pretty well disguising the accent, huh?"

"But I did a background check." Jack kept his voice steady, in control.

Luke smirked. "When you're good, you're good. What can I say?"

Rachel stepped closer to Aidan, inching her way toward him. If Jack could keep Luke talking, she could reach her son.

That's what Jack was trying to tell her. Get Aidan. That's what his look had been for. She felt certain.

She stepped back and her hands felt the rough wood of the stall door prickling her fingertips. If she could just get the door open...

Jack held his hands in the air, as if offering surrender. "You're not going to get away with this, Luke. I'm sure Denton will be here any minute."

"I knocked him out and tied him up. He's no good to you right now."

The latch dropped quietly. Rachel scooted over another step until her fingers felt the crevice between the door and the wall.

"You need to calm down and think this through," Jack said. He glanced again at Rachel, and Rachel saw a slight nod.

"I've done enough thinking to last a lifetime," Luke sneered. "I should have just done away with Rachel when I had the opportunity."

Rachel eased the door open until her hand reached through. She felt Aidan's fingers grip hers. Temporary relief flashed through her. Reaching Aidan was just the beginning. Now they had to get away.

"Why didn't you, Luke? Why did you wait until tonight?"

"There are bigger things at play here, Jack. I thought you would have realized that by now."

Jack nodded ever so slightly toward the barn door. If she was reading him right, he wanted her to run.

"Rachel's parents are the connection. I just haven't figured out why yet. Probably something to do with their work at the Department of Agriculture."

Luke chuckled. "Very good. I underestimated you."

Luke paced toward Jack, and Rachel could see he was caught up in the brilliance of his scheme for a moment, busy giving himself a mental pat on the back. This was her opportunity.

Gripping Aidan's hand, she tugged him forward and swung him into her arms. She then darted toward the door, her legs straining with each step.

"Stop!" Luke shouted.

Rachel looked back in time to see him raise his gun. She sucked in a breath, praying, grasping Aidan more tightly toward her. Just a few more steps and she'd be outside. A few more steps.

She heard a blast, a grunt and then a tumbling sound. She dared another glance back. Jack had tackled Luke. The two struggled. But no one had been shot.

Jack looked over at her, urgency clear in his eyes. "Run, Rachel!"

She reached the grass, ready to run for her life. Then she heard another gunshot.

She looked back. Luke stood above Jack, the gun in his hand. Jack lay on the ground. Was he dead? Her heart ripped in two.

She wanted to stop, to turn around and go back. But Aidan's fingers dug into her neck, reminding her of the other precious life she had to look out for. So she ran. But her heart broke with each step. *Oh, Jack.*

Just as she stepped around the corner, another gunshot rang out.

Tears began rolling down her cheeks.

Luke had finished him off.

TWENTY-SIX

Rachel pushed aside the images that dashed through her mind. Images of Luke finishing off Jack, of him taking a fatal gunshot wound to the heart. She'd have time to mourn later. Right now, she had to get to safety. Luke could come after them any minute.

But Jack...

She wiped away a tear. Jack would want them to get to safety. He'd probably just given his life to ensure that that happened. Rachel couldn't let that sacrifice be in vain.

The house, Rachel thought. She had to get to the house.

But then she'd be putting Jack's parents in danger.

Where did she run? Her gaze darted across the landscape. The farmhouse to her left, the cornfields in front of her, the woods in the distance. Beside the house, there were several vehicles. But she had no vehicle of her own, nor did she have keys to Jack's vehicle.

She didn't know where to go, where to hide.

So she ran toward the woods, limping as she went. She pushed ahead. She'd stay at the woods edge, near the little country lane that ran beside it. At least she wouldn't get swallowed by the foliage that way. The road could be her guide, but the trees would allow her cover.

But Jack...she couldn't stop thinking of Jack. Of his body laying there on the ground in the barn. Had Luke killed him?

Had he died thinking that Rachel blamed him for her husband's death? Because she didn't. She needed to tell him that.

Keep moving, Rachel. Keep moving.

Her back ached. Aidan's forty pounds caused her arms to strain. His death grip on her made it hard to breathe. But she had her son. He was safe. She had to make sure he stayed safe.

She reached the woods, and fear shuddered through her as she looked into the gaping blackness before her. Were there Apaka operatives hiding there? And where was Luke? Was he behind them, just steps away from catching up? She couldn't bring herself to look back, to slow down enough to notice. She had to keep looking forward, to keep moving.

Aidan sniffled in her arms. She wanted to comfort him but couldn't. She had to keep him alive first.

She dodged trees, sprinted through weeds that grabbed at her legs, fought off rocks that threatened to twist her ankles. She moved. Everything blurred around her.

Keep moving. Keep moving. That's what she kept telling herself.

Jack...was Jack dead? Tears burned her eyes at the thought. He couldn't be dead. He'd taken the shot in order to save her life. She wouldn't have escaped without his intervention.

Oh, Jack.

Her breath came in ragged gasps now. Her legs felt like gelatin. All the old wounds from their previous escape through the woods felt raw again, rubbed open in her escape.

Her body demanded that she slow down.

But was that a shout behind her? Was it Luke coming after her?

She heard men talking but couldn't make out their words. All she could think of was Apaka, on their trail.

What would she do? Could she really keep moving? Would

her body hold up? Maybe she should find a hiding place and hunker down until someone found her. But what if that someone were an Apaka operative?

Oh Lord, I don't know what to do. I don't know how much farther I can make it.

Just then she saw headlights flickering down the lane in the distance. Was it help? Or was it the opposite?

She sunk down into a bush, needing to rest for a moment, to gather her thoughts.

The headlights got brighter. The sound of the engine stalled, as if the car had stopped. Her heart nearly stopped also.

"We have to stay quiet, okay?" she whispered to Aidan.

Aidan nodded.

Then she heard a voice calling her. A familiar voice.

"Rachel? Are you out there?"

She stood, relieved that help had come. Someone she knew she could really trust.

"I'm right here."

Jack staggered from the barn and looked in both directions out the door. Where had Rachel gone? Somewhere safe, he prayed. He had to find her. He had to protect her.

He'd checked Luke's heartbeat. He was hanging on, but barely. They needed to get an ambulance out here. Luke might be their only hope of locating Rachel if Apaka got her. He was the only one who held the answers they needed.

Luke hadn't known that Jack carried another gun tucked into his belt. He'd taken Luke by surprise when he pulled it out and got in that shot a split second before Luke had pulled the trigger on Jack. That split second had determined if Jack would live or die.

He had no choice but to live. He had to live to ensure that Rachel was okay.

His gaze roamed his surroundings again. Maybe Rachel had gone back to the house, to the safety offered by his parents. He hoped that's where she'd gone.

If only she'd stayed inside like he'd insisted…but he knew a mother's instinct was strong. She'd gone after her child because, in her mind, she'd had no choice.

A car sped down the lane in the distance. Instinctively, he knew Rachel was inside. He knew Apaka had gotten to her. He had to stop them, but outrunning the car was out of the question.

He reached for his gun and aimed, but everything began to blur around him. Energy seemed to seep from him. His wound must have been worst than he thought. He leaned against the barn to hold his balance. Aiming again, he shot at the car's tires.

He missed. The taillights became mere specks in the distance.

He squinted, trying to see the license plates. It was no use. They were getting away—with Rachel. The thought of someone hurting them crushed his soul.

Grasping his shoulder, Jack started toward the house. He finally reached the back porch, climbed the steps and rapped on the door. His mother's worried face appeared in the window atop the door. The lines around her eyes softened some when she spotted him, and she unlocked the door, pulling him inside.

"You've been shot," she murmured. "Again."

"We've got to find them." Jack pointed to the phone. "I need your keys. I've got to go after them."

His father put an arm around him to help support him. "We've got to get someone to look at you first, son. You're in no state to drive. We've already called the police and the rescue squad."

"They're getting away."

"They're already gone, son." His mother placed a hand on his forearm. "You'll find them. I know you will."

Denton staggered through the back door, his hand atop a knot on his head. His lip was busted, and blood stained his shirt. "Luke. It was Luke. He knocked me out, tied me up." He glanced around the room. "Where are Rachel and Aidan? What happened?"

"Apaka. They got them." Jack clenched his fists in anger.

At that moment, flashing lights sliced through the curtains. The emergency medical squad arrived. Two medics stayed inside to check out Jack's injuries, and two went to the barn for Luke. The medics kept insisting that Jack go to the hospital, but he couldn't stop. Not right now. Instead, they did a temporary bandage on his arm.

He needed the local authorities' help in locating the car that Rachel had gotten into. He could only get that assistance with Vice Admiral Harris's help. He reached for his phone, but it wasn't in his pocket. It must have dropped somewhere. Instead, he grabbed his parents' phone and dialed the vice admiral's number, one he knew by heart. The vice admiral answered on the first ring.

"Jack Sergeant, sir. I need your help. A car picked up Rachel and Aidan. I don't know who was inside or where the car went. I need your help to put out an All Points Bulletin on it."

"What happened?"

Jack explained what he could. Time was ticking away, though. He needed to be out there searching for Rachel himself.

"I'll make a call to the Fayette County sheriff now," Vice Admiral Harris said.

"Thank you." Jack hung up.

He realized he'd never told Vice Admiral Harris that they were in Ohio, though.

* * *

Rachel looked over at her uncle, who sat in the seat beside her. A uniformed man silently drove them away from danger. "I'm glad you got there when you did, Uncle Arnold. You were a real life saver. Luke was working for Apaka. I still can't believe it!"

"I know. We decided to dig a little deeper into the backgrounds of the men at Eyes. After everything that had happened there, we figured someone there was working for the other side. It was just a matter of pinpointing who. I would never have guessed it was Luke."

"So you drove all the way out to Ohio?"

Something flickered across her uncle's face. "I wanted to look into Luke's eyes myself. After all, he used to work for me. It just so happened I arrived when everything went down."

Jack's face flashed in her mind. He'd jumped in front of the bullet to save her. A tear popped into her eye. Her uncle patted her hand.

"It's going to be okay. Everything's going to be okay, dear."

She nodded, wanting to believe him.

They drove for what seemed like forever—it was probably only a few hours in reality, though. In between urgent-sounding phone calls her uncle took regarding the situation, Rachel relayed what had happened, about Jack and Luke and Simon. Finally, they stopped in what seemed like the middle of nowhere. A cabin surrounded by woods in who knows where.

"Another safe house?" When would it end? She wanted Jack near her, protecting her.

Her uncle nodded. "Yes, another safe house. Hopefully this will be the last one."

They stepped inside the cabin, which already had guards,

barred windows, a security system and multiple locks on the door.

"I think you'll be comfortable here," her uncle said. "We have a room especially designed for your safety."

Comfortable? She doubted it. It was just another prison. How long would she be at this one?

Her uncle walked to a door located on the back wall of the house, inserted a key and pushed it open. "Why don't you check your new space out?"

Rachel nodded. Holding Aidan's hand, she stepped forward. The room was larger than she'd expected, with no windows. A couch sat at the center of the space. Rachel was surprised to see the back of two heads there. There were other people staying at the safe house?

Rachel paused, something oddly familiar about them. Her heart played an odd beat and she rubbed her eyes a moment. She had to be seeing things. She stepped closer.

"Mom? Dad?"

TWENTY-SEVEN

"Rachel? Aidan?" her mom whispered.

Rachel flew across the room and into her mother's arms. Her dad joined them, wrapping his arms around them both.

Rachel pulled back and held them both at arm's length. Time had taken a small toll on them. Both looked grayer, thinner, paler. But they were alive. "I can't believe it's you. That you're here. That you're alive."

Her dad pulled her into another hug. "Oh, Rachel. I never thought I'd see you again."

"I didn't think I'd see you either. I thought…I thought…" All at once, she remembered the day she got the news of her parents' accident. The police officer at her door, their bodies burned beyond recognition, their double funeral.

Her mother's face twisted into a frown. "I know."

Rachel stepped back and shook her head, trying desperately to comprehend everything that was happening. "I don't understand."

Her mother's frown deepened. Her mom and dad looked at each other, grimaces across their features. Before they could say anything else, a shadow filled the doorway.

"You'll have plenty of time to catch up," Uncle Arnold said. His once comforting face now looked menacing with his wrinkled forehead and a smile slightly curling one side of his mouth.

Rachel's eyes narrowed. "What's going on? I don't understand. You knew, Uncle Arnold? This whole time you knew they were alive and you didn't tell me?"

He smiled, but the action didn't reach his eyes. "I'm sorry, Rachel. There were just other more important things at stake."

Weren't those the exact words that Luke had used earlier?

Rachel grabbed Aidan and backed up, away from her uncle. "You work for Apaka?"

His smile slipped some. "You could say that."

"How could you work for them? They're trying to kill me. They kill innocent people every day. And you…you work for the Department of Defense. I thought you loved your country." Rachel looked back at her parents, begging for a sign of understanding. What was going on? Why were her parents still alive? Nothing made sense.

Uncle Arnold glanced at his watch. "I actually have some things I need to tend to back in Washington. I'll be back in the morning. 6:00 a.m." His gaze cut to her parents. "You'll have until then to decide whether you're going to give me the information I want. If not…" He looked at Rachel and smiled. The message was loud and clear: If not, she would die.

He stepped from the room and a lock clicked in place. They were all stuck in this tiny, windowless room. Rachel looked at her parents, confusion and fear colliding inside. "What's going on?"

Vice Admiral Harris had been involved this entire time? He was the true inside man. Simon had just been a cover-up. Luke had just been a henchman.

How could Jack not have seen it?

The better question was, how was he going to discover where Rachel was? He'd bet anything that Vice Admiral Harris had her and Aidan. But where would he take them?

"What do you want to do? Your call. I'm behind you, whatever you decide," Denton said.

"I can't call the Department of Defense. No one will take my word over the vice admiral's." Even to Jack, the story seemed far-fetched.

He glanced at his watch, his shoulder still throbbing. He knew that every second counted. He needed a plan and he needed it now. First, he needed to call his contact with the FBI. Where had he left his phone? Had it fallen out in the barn?

"What's wrong?"

"My phone. I can't find it. It must have fallen out somewhere."

"Last time I saw it, Aidan was playing with it."

The boy loved to play games with the various apps he had on the device. What if Aidan had taken his phone, slipped it into his back pocket maybe? Would Rachel realize that the phone was there? Would she call for help?

Better yet…Jack had just installed a new app that would trace his phone's location. If he could figure out where his phone was, he could figure out where Rachel and Aidan were.

Rachel squeezed her mom's hand as they sat beside each other on the ratty couch. Aidan nearly bounced out of her lap, he had so much pent-up energy. She prayed for patience before turning back to her parents.

"So, the car accident was just a cover-up?"

"Arnold was behind it all." Her mom wiped away a tear and hugged Aidan to her again. "He even placed some old cadavers in the vehicle so no one would suspect anything."

Rachel shook her head. "Why would he do that? I still don't understand."

Her parents looked at each other again, sharing that

concerned expression that hadn't left their faces since she'd arrived in this cabin.

Her dad cleared his throat. "Arnold put us in charge of a joint government-authorized project with the Department of Agriculture and the Department of Defense. It was all top secret, on a need-to-know basis."

"What was it?" Rachel considered herself need-to-know right now.

Her mom took over the story. "We developed a super bug that would destroy crops in other countries. In one day, this insect could wipe fields clean, leaving countries that were in opposition to the United States with nothing to eat. It would destroy their economy, make them more likely to bow to the demands of countries like the U.S."

"At first we thought the U.S. would only use this bug as a bargaining chip for countries that were in the middle of terrible humanitarian crises," her dad said. "We thought the government would use it to benefit the hurting and the helpless. But we learned that certain people planned on using it to have the upper hand with countries for other reasons, reasons that were less than noble."

Her mom nodded sadly. "And besides that, there was always the risk that the bug wouldn't die in twenty-four hours, that it would evolve and really spread to be a world crisis. You just can't rely on guesses when it comes to things of this nature. It could destroy life as we know it."

"And imagine what it would do if the wrong people got their hands on it?" Her father leaned back into the couch, as if the idea still made him weary. "If someone set that bug loose in the United States, it would destroy all of our crops within a week's period. We'd be left with nothing to eat. It would be a terrorist's dream."

Her mom's eyes lit with fire and she sliced her hands through the air. "That's when we decided that we couldn't do it. We couldn't release the information to the government that we had spent months and months and millions of dollars to develop. We burned all of the information and made sure that no one would ever put the pieces together again."

"Your uncle didn't like that, I can assure you. We got into so many fights about it." Her dad leaned forward now, his elbows on his knees. His eyes looked sad, tired.

Rachel searched through her memories for anything that would hint that all of this was going on. "I do seem to recall that you all weren't speaking very much in the months before the accident. I guess that was why."

Her mother nodded. "It was. We didn't know that your uncle was working for Apaka. He wanted to sell that information to them for a large price—just as he'd been selling other government secrets to them for a very, very long time."

"That's how he could afford all of his houses." The truth permeated Rachel's thoughts.

"The price tag he would have gotten for this super bug would have been out of this world." Her dad shook his head. "There's not a price tag you can put on a human life, though."

Rachel sucked in a deep breath, trying to comprehend everything. "I don't understand—why does he hate the United States so much?" She looked at her father for an answer, since the two had been college roommates.

"His own father was killed in battle. His mother used to hate war. I think he grew up listening to her talk about the evils of the United States and it just kind of became ingrained in him. But he learned to cover up his distain. He figured out that the best way to get revenge on the country was to get on the inside. He could do the most damage that way. And that's what he's been doing."

Rachel let go of her mother's hand and rubbed her hands against her legs. She needed to fill her parents in on everything that happened leading up to this moment. "There's been a list. My name was on it. Everyone else is dead."

Her mother's face took on a burdened look, her eyes closing and her eyebrows pinching together. "Everyone on that list was connected to us. Most of them were people who helped us formulate the bug. We never told them the truth about what we were creating, but we always had covers using our jobs at the Department of Agriculture. They had no idea. Your uncle was trying to convince us to recreate the bug. He said if we didn't, he'd kill the people on the list."

Her mother dabbed tears from her eyes. "We didn't know what to do. We didn't want to see innocent people die, but we kept thinking about the greater good. Millions would die if he got his hands on that information."

Her dad squeezed her hand. "And then he put your name on the list. I don't think he really wanted to kill you. I think in some twisted way he does care about you. But he's threatening to kill you if we don't give him the information."

Her mom looked up, strain in her eyes. "He won't kill us, because without us, he'll never get the information he wants. That's why he keeps threatening us, trying to find the last straw that will break our backs."

"And come tomorrow morning, he might discover that he's finally found our one weakness." Her dad shook his head, his voice cracking. "I just never thought he'd sink low enough to actually harm you or Aidan. Now I fear he's desperate enough that he will. I just can't bear the thought of that."

TWENTY-EIGHT

"**I**'ve got the coordinates of your cell phone!" Denton explained.

Jack rushed to the computer and saw a map on the screen. A red star indicated the location of his cell phone. "West Virginia?" he muttered. "It looks like they're in the middle of nowhere. There's not even a marked road leading to their location."

"It would appear," Denton agreed.

"Figure out how far away that is from here."

"Already done. It's three hours from here, approximately."

Jack glanced at the clock above the kitchen table and saw it was already past midnight. He wanted to work quickly before they changed locations again. That didn't give him any time to mobilize any of his men to help, though. For now, it would just be him and Denton. He had no idea what they were going up against, either.

"Jack—" his mother started. She stepped behind him, wringing her hands. Her eyes were wrinkled with fear.

He kissed her cheek. "I'll be careful. I promise."

Before she could argue anymore, he and Denton flew out the door. They had to get to Rachel and Aidan before Vice Admiral Harris wiped them off his hit list for good.

Denton drove so Jack could rest his shoulder more. Jack eyed their location on the map, his mind racing with possibilities. He'd considered calling his cell phone. But what if the vice admiral didn't know Aidan had the phone? If Jack called and the ringing phone alerted him to the device, they could lose their one lifeline. So he didn't call. He waited instead.

It was hard enough to believe that Vice Admiral Harris was involved somehow with Apaka, but it was even harder to imagine him putting Rachel and Aidan in danger. Maybe Rachel was right and her parents were the connection. His best guess would be that they were working on some kind of secret project. Maybe it had gotten them in trouble? Were all of the people on the list somehow connected to that project?

Denton drummed his fingers on the steering wheel as the night stretched on before them. "Any idea what we're up against when we get to wherever it is we're going?"

"Not a clue. They're in the middle of nowhere. Who knows how many men might be there or what kind of state Rachel and Aidan will be in. I can only pray that they're not harmed." He couldn't even think about any other possibility.

"Why would Vice Admiral Harris be involved with this?"

Jack shared his theory.

"But what would threatening people who helped out with this secret project accomplish? And why Rachel? It's not like she's going to know anything about her parents' work."

"It almost seems like they're trying to find out information."

"Maybe they're marking off people until they get the answer they want." But again, why would Rachel be on the list? She knew nothing. Why would her uncle not kill her when he'd killed the rest? "Denton, go faster. I have a bad feeling about this."

Rachel watched the minutes tick by on her watch. Aidan rested with his head in her lap. They sat on the ratty couch.

Her parents sat across from them on a cot. Strain showed on their pinched faces. She still couldn't believe that she was seeing them alive. It seemed impossible, like part dream, part nightmare.

She stroked Aidan's hair. "Have you been here for four years?" She glanced around the bland room and couldn't imagine being here for that long.

Her dad leaned forward, elbows on his knees. "No, they've moved us a few times."

"No chance of getting away?"

Her mother shook her head. "No, none. Not at our age. It's so secluded everywhere we've been. Even if we could get out of the house, the wilderness would claim us. There's no one around for miles. They made sure that we knew that."

Rachel's heart broke for her parents. This must have been torture for them.

Torture.

Her heart felt like it stopped at the thought. "Did they hurt you?" She hardly wanted to ask the question.

Her dad reached over and squeezed her hand. "No, they've fed us and taken care of us. It could have been worse."

Rachel had that to be thankful for, but still, things didn't seem like they could be much worst right now. "How many men do they have guarding the place?"

"Usually four. All armed. There's no way of escaping, Rachel. Believe me. We've had four years to think about every possibility."

Rachel released Aidan from her lap and let him run around the room. Then she stood. "There's got to be a way out. We could make a run for it. Anything would be better than just sitting here and waiting. I'll be with you. Even if you had to hide out in the woods, I could run and get help. Send them back for you. There's got to be something we can do."

"Everyone thinks we're dead, Rachel." Her mother's emotionless expression made Rachel's heart thud with sadness…and fear.

Not everyone thought Rachel was dead. Jack wouldn't give up until he found her.

Unless he was dead.

Her heart thudded with sadness.

Denton would look for them then. He would pick up where Jack had left off. But how would he ever find them out here? How would anyone find them? Her parents were right. They'd been here for four years. If no one had found them yet, why would they find them now?

Rachel remembered Jack's mother's words, about how love required risk. Yes, it did. Life required risk. Once she'd become a mom, all other risks had taken a backseat. All she'd wanted was to be safe.

But right now, all she wanted was Jack. She could live with his job, his work. She just wanted him, wanted to feel his arms around her.

And she wanted out from this cabin. She felt along the walls, searching for something, anything.

"We've done that, Rachel," her dad said. "There's nothing. The only way in or out of this room is through that door, that has five locks on the other side. And the men… Two are inside, two are outside. They bring us food at 8:00 a.m., noon and 6:00 p.m."

Rachel guessed that's what they'd learned while doing the same thing every day for four years. Her mother's paleness was worrisome. She needed to see a doctor. And her father looked frailer than she remembered. The bags under his eyes spoke of his sleepless nights.

"I'm not going to sit here and wait for them to kill me in front of you," Rachel muttered. She stared at the door, trying to formulate a plan.

* * *

"That's got to be the road leading to the property there." Jack pointed to an overgrown path that veered off of the treacherous mountain road they'd been traveling down for the past twenty minutes.

Denton pulled to a stop in front of it. "That appears to be a locked gate and a No Trespassing sign."

"We'll park and hike in. We can't exactly rumble up the driveway and announce our arrival, now, can we?"

Denton looked at the GPS. "According to this map, it's a good six-mile hike still to get there…if this is the correct location."

"We don't have any other choice." Jack had called an old friend at the FBI to let him know what was going on. He told him the whole story, as well as he knew it, so that if anything happened to him and Denton, someone else would know to look for Rachel and Aidan…and Vice Admiral Harris.

"The night will be on our side, at least," Denton said. "No one should see us coming."

They found a neglected roadside pull-off with a couple of faded picnic tables. Denton pulled over, inching as close to the woods as possible. The two men hopped from the SUV and began gathering branches to place over the vehicle and conceal it. No need of giving themselves away in case anyone drove past.

Jack's arm still ached. He needed additional medical treatment. The bullet hadn't done any real damage, but he'd need to have it looked at again. It wasn't the top thing on his priority list now, but as he pulled his holster over his shoulder, his body protested. He pushed aside the pain. All he had to do was think about Rachel and Aidan, and his focus returned. He hadn't realized how much they'd begun to feel like a family to him. This went beyond his job. He wanted to protect them because he'd grown to love them.

They stayed in the woods but followed beside the road for their journey up the mountain. The hike would tax them, even if they were well rested and uninjured. They needed to keep a steady pace to preserve their energy for when they arrived wherever they were going.

Jack's cell phone—actually, his father's, since Aidan apparently had his—buzzed. Without missing a step, he pulled it from his belt and answered. It was his FBI contact.

"I looked into Vice Admiral Harris's properties. He does have one in West Virginia. It was hard to trace back to him because he keeps the deed under his father's name. It appears to be at the GPS coordinates you sent me."

"Tell me about the property."

"3,000 square feet. Two stories. No basement. It's surrounded by miles and miles of nothing. If I had more time I could get a floor plan."

"How about a satellite image of it?"

"I'm looking at it right now. I see two men outside of the house. They appear to be armed. There's one car parked in front of it. That's all I see right now."

"Perfect. Thanks, Justin."

Jack relayed the information to Denton as they continued their climb. The darkness was beginning to disappear, and the sky was becoming more of a murky gray than black. They had to pick up the pace. Jack couldn't risk losing their cover of darkness.

More important, he couldn't risk losing the two people he'd come to love.

TWENTY-NINE

Rachel plopped back down on the couch, after trying to find an exit with no luck. Her mom and dad were right—there was no getting out of this place except through the door. The problem was that an armed guard stood on the other side.

Aidan began stirring from the other end of the couch. She smiled at her son and stroked his hair away from his face.

"Hey, buddy."

His sleepy gaze scanned the place. "Are we still here?"

Rachel nodded. "Hopefully not much longer." Even as she said the words, she realized her hope had begun to fade. At 6:00 a.m., her uncle had promised to come and finish her off. What would happen to her sweet son?

Aidan sighed. "I'm bored."

"You just woke up, sweetie."

He sighed again. "I want Mr. Jack."

Rachel's heart lurched. "I know, honey. Me, too."

"Is it okay if I play a game, Mommy?"

"Absolutely."

Aidan reached into his pocket and pulled out a cell phone. Rachel sat up straighter, her eyes widening. "Aidan, what is that?"

His cheeks reddened. "I know I shouldn't have taken it. I was going to give it back, but I didn't have the chance. Please don't be mad."

Rachel's heart skipped a beat. "I'm not mad, Aidan, even though you shouldn't take things that don't belong to you. We'll talk about that later. For now, do you mind if I look at Mr. Jack's cell phone?"

He shook his head and handed it to her. Her hands trembled as she held it. This could be the answer she'd been praying for. She could only hope they had a signal.

She held the button down to turn the phone on. The screen lit up. The first thing she saw was the time. 5:00 a.m. Only one more hour.

Her throat was dry as she swallowed.

The signal bar showed they had reception here. Slight, but they had it. She let out a soft squeal.

Her parents stirred.

"What is it, Mom?" Aidan leaned over to see the phone.

Her dad lifted his head from the pillow and blinked several times. "What's going on?"

"Aidan has a cell phone."

"A cell phone? At his age?" her mom said.

"That's not the point right now. The point is that we have reception." Who should she call? 911? Would dispatch even believe her? And how would she explain where she was? There was only one hour until Uncle Arnold returned.

She found Jack's contacts. Who could she call, if not Jack himself? Was Jack even around to call? Her heart fell at the thought. She remembered his seemingly lifeless body but fought to not give into despair.

She found the number for Jack's parents. On a prayer, she hit Call. Before the first ring was complete, Jack's dad answered. "Jack?"

"Mr. Sergeant, this is Rachel."

"Rachel? Are you okay?" A mixture of relief and concern sounded in his voice.

"I guess you could say I'm okay. How's Jack, Mr. Sergeant?"

"He's okay."

"He's alive?"

"And kicking."

Relief washed through her, but only for a moment. "Mr. Sergeant, my uncle has kidnapped us. My parents are alive. And I don't know who to call for help. My uncle's going to be back to kill me in an hour."

"Call my cell phone."

"Your cell phone?"

"Jack has it, and he's on his way to find you."

Her heart soared. Of course Jack was on his way to find her. That was Jack. How could she think any less?

She skipped the formalities and ended the call, only to immediately find the contact on Jack's phone list and hit Call. A moment later, she heard a surprised, "Hello?"

"Jack?"

"Rachel?"

"I've never been so glad to hear your voice."

"Ditto. I'll have more than that to say later. Right now, I need to know where you are."

"We're in some cabin in the middle of nowhere."

"Do you know how many men are there guarding you?"

"We think there are four. Two outside, two inside."

"Where are you in the house? Do you know?"

"It's a room in the middle of the house. No windows. I'm guessing that maybe it was a bedroom at one time and they walled part of it up."

"Where's your uncle?"

"He's going to be back at six. He said he's going to—"

"I need you to hold tight, Rachel. I'm on my way."

"Okay." She paused, her thoughts racing. "Jack?"

"Don't say it."

"How do you know what I'm going to say?"

"You're going to say something that you might not say if you didn't fear that you could die. I want to hear it when you're safe and sound. Can you wait an hour?"

Rachel smiled. An hour. She'd love nothing more than to tell Jack how she really felt then. She only prayed she survived long enough to do just that.

Jack had never been so relieved to hear anyone's voice. Good old Aidan. Sure, he needed a lesson about taking things that didn't belong to him, but this would be the one time he wouldn't get a lecture from Jack. His sticky hands had possibly saved their lives.

Denton looked at the GPS in his hands. "We should be coming right up on it, Jack."

No sooner had the words left his mouth then they heard a vehicle rumbling up the lane. Vice Admiral Harris. Rachel's words rung in his ears. He would kill her at 6:00 a.m. He glanced at his watch. They still had thirty minutes.

The cabin came into view. They circled the house and saw the two men stationed outside. They also saw Vice Admiral Harris getting out of the car and striding up to the front door. They had to work quickly.

"I'll take the guy by the back door, you take the other one," Jack instructed.

Denton nodded and they split up. Jack crept around the building, trying to get a better view of his target. The man, short but wiry, looked rather bored at his post, his gaze often roaming his surroundings and checking his cell phone. As soon as the man began to punch in some text on his phone, Jack swiftly moved toward him.

The man struggled, but Jack put him in a sleeper hold. As soon as the man passed out, Jack grabbed some duct tape from his backpack and tied the man up. Just as Jack finished, Denton came around the corner.

"You ready to move inside?" Denton whispered.

"Let's do it."

"There's one man by the front door. He's armed. The other guard must be in front of the room where they're keeping Rachel and Aidan. I don't know where the vice admiral is."

"Probably with Rachel." Jack glanced at the door. "Here's what we'll do. I'll keep an eye on the guard by the door while you pick the lock. We'll take him out before the other guard even knows it."

"Got it." Denton bent by the front door and, using a kit from the backpack, quietly unlocked the door.

Jack kept watch from around the corner. He could see the guard standing by the door. At just the right time, they'd slip inside and take him out. They had their chance when he stepped toward the table and started ruffling through a magazine. Jack nodded toward Denton.

Quietly, Denton opened the door and slipped inside. In less than two minutes, the guard was knocked out and tied up.

Voices came from down the hall. One was headed their way. Jack slipped into a closet while Denton hunkered behind a couch. They waited until the right moment.

"You got that right," one of the guards said, approaching the living room. Jack tuned his ear to the voice, listening as the man approached. "Where did Will go? Will?"

Jack threw open the closet door and tackled the man. The guard's gun clattered to the floor. Denton grabbed it and aimed it at the guard. Before he could say anything else, Jack used the duct tape to subdue him also.

"What was that sound?" The vice admiral's voice got louder as he came down the hallway. "I'm ready for you in the other room, Will."

Jack dragged the guards out of the vice admiral's line of

sight. Then he waited. As soon as the vice admiral stepped into the room, Jack stepped out with his gun aimed right at him.

The vice admiral's eyebrow twitched in disdain. "Well, if it isn't Jack Sergeant. I shouldn't be surprised to see you here. You always were persistent."

Despite his throbbing shoulder, Jack held the gun steady. "I wouldn't make any sudden moves, sir. I don't want to take you down, but I will."

The vice admiral chuckled, not looking a bit ruffled by Jack's appearance. "You think anyone will believe your word over mine? It's doubtful. You have no proof that I've done anything. And you won't have any proof. I assure you. I'm very good at what I do. I've been doing it for thirty years and haven't been caught yet. If you think I'm going to let you ruin things for me, you're wrong."

"Put your weapon down, sir."

"I have nothing to lose, Jack." The vice admiral reached into his pocket and pulled out a gun. His eyes gleamed as he raised the weapon and aimed it at Jack.

Rachel heard the commotion from the other room. Was that Jack? It had to be. Jack was here. He would rescue them.

She stepped toward the door, every cell in her body screaming with fear and hope.

"What are you doing, Rachel?" Her mom grabbed her arm. "You can't go out there. They all have guns."

"I've got to see if I can help." Rachel twisted the door handle. It turned. Her heart leapt into her throat.

Her mom covered her mouth with her hand, worry staining every feature of her face. "Be careful, Rachel."

"Mommy?" Aidan tugged at her shirt.

"Stay with Grandma and Grandpa. Okay? No arguments." Rachel crept down the hallway, toward the voices. They were talking in the front room. One of the voices was clearly Jack's.

"There are two of us against you, sir. If you try to take one of us out, the other one can still shoot you. It would be wise to simply put the gun down and turn yourself in. The FBI are on their way."

"You won't take me alive. I can promise you that." Even without seeing her uncle's face, Rachel could imagine the sneer he wore. She'd seen it herself too many times.

"This doesn't have to get any worse than it already is."

Her uncle chuckled. "Do you know what the authorities will do to me? They'll charge me with treason. My name and picture will be all over the news. I'll bring shame to my family."

"You should have thought about that before you joined up with Apaka."

Rachel looked up and saw a fifth guard standing on the second-story balcony, where Jack couldn't see him. He crouched, his gun aimed at Jack.

"Jack, behind you!" Rachel shouted.

Jack swung his gun up just as the shooter fired. Uncle Arnold turned his gun toward her. She ducked. Shots were fired. The smell of gun smoke filled the room. Rachel's mom screamed from the other room.

Rachel stood and lowered her hands from her ears. She saw Uncle Arnold on the floor, a wound at his knee. The shooter from upstairs lay on the ground and Denton hurried up the steps to him.

Rachel stepped over her uncle, kicking the gun out of the way in the process. She ran into Jack's arms.

"You're okay."

"I'm more than okay now." His arms encircled her and he pulled her tightly toward him.

Just as her parents and Aidan stepped out of the room, sirens sounded outside.

"Jack, I'd like for you to meet my parents."

THIRTY

Rachel knocked on the door to the hospital room. A cranky "come in" sounded from the other side. She took Aidan's hand and pushed the door open. Jack sat in his hospital bed, a scowl on his face and a bandage across his shoulder.

As soon as Jack spotted them, his eyes lit up. "I was afraid you were my doctor again, telling me I wasn't ready to go home."

Aidan scrambled away from Rachel and began climbing in bed beside Jack. "Mr. Jack, Mr. Jack—"

Rachel reached for him. "Aidan—"

Jack held up a hand. "It's okay." Aidan scrambled beside him in bed and looked up at him, his eyes glowing.

Rachel smiled with relief and lowered herself at his bedside. She took Jack's hand in hers. "How are you?"

"I'll be better once they let me get out of here."

"They just released Aidan and me. My parents haven't been discharged yet. Doctors want to do a few more tests on them."

"Hospitals like to do that."

Rachel reached into her purse and plucked something out. "This is for you." She handed Jack an envelope.

His eyes glittered in curiosity as he gingerly took it from her. "For me?"

"For you."

"From…?"

Rachel smiled. "Me."

"Can I read it now?"

"Please do." She rested her hands in her lap, waiting with anticipation for him to read the words she'd crafted to him. "Since letters are kind of what I'm known for, I thought it was only appropriate that I write you one."

He gently opened the flap and pulled out the neatly folded piece of stationery inside. Rachel had handwritten this one on her favorite paper. Jack glanced up at her again before turning his gaze back to the words before him.

He cleared his throat and began reading aloud. "'Jack, I shouldn't feel safe with you. Your job is dangerous. But your job is also much needed and one that keeps our country safe. The truth is that I feel safer with you than I ever have with anyone. I like how Aidan and I feel like a family with you, like you were meant to be a part of our lives. I'll never forget the way you jumped in front of that bullet for us. You showed us time and time again that you would give your life for us, and for that I am grateful beyond words. Thank you, Jack Sergeant, for being selfless, loyal and kind, for being a father figure to Aidan, a confidante to me, and for helping me to believe in love again.'" He looked up, emotion tearing in his eyes. "Thank you, Rachel. Can you ever forgive me for Andrew?"

She gently touched his cheek. "There's nothing to forgive. You didn't plant the IED on the side of the road, Jack. There's nothing to blame you for."

"You're a very generous woman, Rachel."

"I don't know about that. I know I am grateful, though. I don't know how we'll ever repay you for all you've done."

He grabbed her hand, his eyes intense. "There is one way."

Rachel felt heat rush to her cheeks. "What's that?"

"You could marry me. Make me a part of your family. I can't imagine living life without the two of you."

"Say yes, Mommy. Say yes!" Aidan said, bouncing on the bed. "I want Mr. Jack to live with us forever."

Jack and Rachel laughed. Rachel's laughter faded as she looked into Jack's eyes. "Was that a proposal, Mr. Sergeant?"

"I'd get down on one knee if I could."

She squeezed his hand. "I'd be honored."

He let out a whoop, just as Aidan threw himself over Jack's chest in a hug. Rachel wished she could do the same, but she restrained herself. There'd be time for that later.

"What's all the commotion in here?"

Rachel looked back in time to see her parents enter the room.

"Rachel just agreed to marry me. If that's okay with you, sir." Jack looked at Rachel's dad.

"Rachel has told us all about you." Her dad grinned and reached over to shake Jack's hand. "It would be an honor to have you as part of our family."

"I was hoping that maybe Operation 26 Letters would team up with Eyes. I think we'd make a nice team. What do you say? I even have some office space you can use at our headquarters."

"I think that sounds perfect."

Jack looked past Rachel at her parents. "And you can bet that I'm not letting her out of my sight. Aidan, either."

Rachel squeezed his hand again. "I'm not complaining. In fact, there's nowhere else I'd rather be than with you and Aidan."

Jack brushed her cheek with his hand. "I love you, Rachel Reynolds."

Rachel smiled, tears of joy rushing to her eyes. "I love you, too, Jack Sergeant."

* * * * *

Dear Reader,

"I Love Jet Noise" is a popular saying often found on bumper stickers where I live.

I do love jet noise because, to me, the sound reminds me of the freedoms I have and those who have fought to give me those freedoms.

I live in an area of Virginia where I hear a lot of jet noise coming from the military bases all around the region. I have many friends who serve the country through the armed forces. I'm so privileged to be able to see their dedication to our country and the sacrifices they make daily. Each of them inspires me.

If you know someone in the military, I encourage you to send them a letter, just like Rachel does in *The Last Target*. Let them know how much you appreciate them and their service to our country.

Blessings!
Christy Barritt

Questions for Discussion

1. Rachel Reynolds likes to encourage those in the military. We all need encouragement sometimes. Is there anyone you can encourage this week?

2. The Bible says in Proverbs that the right word at the right times is like a piece of custom-made jewelry (Message Version). Is there a time when you were down and someone's encouragement lifted you?

3. Rachel tells Jack that if she succeeds or if she fails, it's all a part of God's plan. Success in God's eyes is different from success in the world's eyes. Do you ever find yourself buying into the world's lies about success? What is God's definition of success?

4. Rachel said that she long ago stopped asking why life wasn't fair and that she'd come to the conclusion that despite life not being fair, God was still good. Sometimes it's hard to separate our view of life from our view of God. We see negative things going on around us and we lose sight of God's sovereignty. What are some things we can do to direct our gazes back to God when this happens?

5. Rachel tells Jack that God is the one who can lift our burdens. When was there a time that you felt burdened? Why? What made you realize you had to give your burdens over to God? Was it easy? How did you feel afterward?

6. Rachel comes to the conclusion that God can take the bad things in our lives and turn them into something

beautiful. Is there anything tragic that's happened in your life that you can turn around into a ministry to others?

7. Jack is still holding on to guilt for his past mistakes, so much that he won't allow himself any pleasure in the present. Is there any guilt that you're holding on to that you've asked for forgiveness for but have trouble letting go of?

8. John 15:13 tells us, "Greater love hath no man than this, that a man lay down his life for friends." This can be said of those who have died serving our country, but it can also be said of Jesus Christ, who gave His life for us. How does this realization change your daily life?

9. Rachel realizes just how important family is in her life once she's left virtually alone. Is family important to you? What's one way you can show your family how important they are to you today?

10. Rachel, at times throughout the book, fears that her days are numbered as the terrorists close in. How would you change the way you lived if you thought tomorrow might never come?

INSPIRATIONAL

Inspirational romances to warm your heart & soul.

TITLES AVAILABLE NEXT MONTH

Available October 11, 2011

NIGHTWATCH
The Defenders
Valerie Hansen

THE CAPTAIN'S MISSION
Military Investigations
Debby Giusti

PRINCESS IN PERIL
Reclaiming the Crown
Rachelle McCalla

FREEZING POINT
Elizabeth Goddard

LISCNM0911

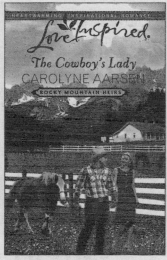